PRAISE FOR *NEW MISTAKES*

"I've never read anything like this. Goldberg writes with such louche charm that you end up compelled to read in an ever-faster shuffle of swoons, amusement, and awe at the fantastical moves that *New Mistakes* pulls off."
　　—Torrey Peters, author of *Detransition, Baby*

"I couldn't put this book down! Goldberg's writing is packed with humor that is precise, profound, and inventive. A master of blending science fiction and queer life, *New Mistakes* is a gift to the literary world. This book is exactly what we need right now."
　　—Julián Delgado Lopera, author of *Fiebre Tropical*

"*New Mistakes*, this is it, this is the thing, this is where we are, the sex and the trouble, the thrill and the comedown, the grabby joy and the grubby desolation, amped up, falling down, zipping on over, friendship and loss, family and desperation, choice and destiny, fireworks in the smoggy sky."
　　—Daniel Handler, author of *A Series of Unfortunate Events*

"Clement reinvents a holy Wildean wit that cuts deep with their particular medicine of tenderness and the high stakes of the heart. An emo pop sci-fi hangout of the highest order."
　　—Bett Williams, author of *Girl Walking Backwards*

Published by DOPAMINE
1139 N Summit Ave Pasadena, CA 91103
www.dopaminepress.org

Special thanks to Katie Fricas

Cover Design: Faye Orlove
Layout: Hedi El Kholti

ISBN: 978-1-63590-225-9

Distributed by the MIT Press, Cambridge, Mass. and London, England
Printed in the United States of America

10 9 8 7 6 5 4 3 2 1

NEW MISTAKES

Clement Goldberg

DOPAMINE
BOOKS AND PRINTED MATTER

For Michelle Tea

1

Julia woke up like a piece of sweaty sandwich meat. Her eyes were stuck to the nape of her dewy girlfriend Reggie, and the back of her legs adhered to an accidental boyfriend whose van they all called home since trimming weed together in Northern California. Julia chalked the decision to open up their relationship to the fact that they had been perpetually high for months. Now, she was over a month late to house sit for her half-brother, but mere exits away from keeping her word. Julia had to pee. She kissed her girlfriend's shoulder and slipped free without waking them. She grabbed a pair of cut-off shorts and a balled-up t-shirt then quietly exited the passenger seat. She was still in love with her girlfriend and maybe even the tiniest bit in love with her boyfriend too.

Rest stop parking lots can go either way; this one was blissfully quiet and a bit too bright. Not much foot traffic. Julia saw some cute yellow wildflowers on her way into the restroom. The flowers were so adorable that she plucked a handful. Unsure if it was because of all the sex she was having, the triangle-shaped bouquet made her think of pubic hair. She unzipped the front of her shorts and placed the flowers. It would have been sexy to have them sticking out of her panties like unshaven hairs, but she wasn't wearing any underwear. She had to work for the right bush. She shaped and arranged the flowers just so, then she photographed herself from a number of angles, unsure if she should include more of her body in the frame.

A random soccer mom desperate to share a look of disgust waited on Julia to notice her. Julia did not care how she felt and, without looking up from her phone, let her know that by saying "What." with a hard period. Julia was reluctant to turn off airplane mode, but the cell service was terrible anyway, so it didn't matter. Her half-brother Franklin sometimes tried to call her for an update but eventually resigned to firing off text flares, in hopes of any kind of response. He had been incredibly generous for a new figure in her life, their relationship beginning in earnest only a year ago. Julia's mother was the younger second wife to Franklin's father and Julia's birth marked Franklin's exit. She was already letting him down, but he did not know it, like a tree falling in the forest. She only had to duck his calls for a short while longer. Most troubling was the terrible phone reception that prevented Julia from sending her lovers thirst traps. She would have to bring them wildflower bouquets instead.

Julia did not know that when the van door shut behind her, the two bodies still inside had gotten busy with their own phone cameras. Dressed only in balaclavas, the pair were weeks into making sex-in-public videos they uploaded to an amateur porn site under the handle *pussy_bloc*. It was Reggie's idea, and she didn't tell Julia about it because then it would have become an art project. Reggie just wanted to get plowed in a sundress like everyone else. She was sharing a similar thought aloud as Julia made it back to the van. Just inside the open door, Julia heard their shared boyfriend, "I only want to be with you. Can we please just break up with her already?" Reggie had hoped to maintain throuplehood at least until she had tired of the proper bed and clawfoot bathtub at Franklin's house. She was so close she could smell the freshly laundered linens.

Julia should have said something, anything, to let them know she was standing within earshot. There was a decent amount of self-harm in her decision to eavesdrop. It was almost too predictable how painful it was. Her heart met the business end of the Three of Swords as she rounded the parking space. In a series of loud rapid-fire swooshes, Julia was impaled by an onslaught of text messages from Franklin. It surprised all three of them, and Julia made a split-second decision to keep things close to her chest. It was almost satisfying once she decided what came next. Julia extended her bouquets to the eager recipients: a boy toy in a man-bun and doe-eyed Reggie with her dainty septum ring, then released the delicate flowers just shy of the outstretched hands in wait, crushing the petals under her sneakers. She boarded the van, put on her sunglasses and hoodie for the fallout.

Reggie remained outside but in the threshold. She was in triage mode, reciting passages from a non-violent communication work-shop in manic free verse. Julia lit a joint and put on headphones. The van doors flanked an impromptu outdoor theater. Julia, its lone audience member, watched on as a man-baby gloated under a veneer of self-flagellation. He patted his own back and cried, "Ouch." Julia did not hear a word that either stage performer uttered, but it was plain to see that they were both phoning it in. How insulting. Julia stubbed the joint, leapt from the van, and shoved him backwards. She mumble-yelled, "Go take your victory lap, you needy dickface." Julia was about to push him into the parking lot, but Reggie held her back. She whispered, "What are your needs" over and over. Reggie tugged on Julia's earlobe and kissed her neck while holding her tight against her chest. The unexpected affection snapped Julia back into her body, the last place she wanted to be.

"I need you to drop me off at my brother's house."

His top knot cocked like a dog's ear as he asked Reggie if the two of them could check in to make sure that it was safe to drive the wild child in his van. Reggie rolled her eyes. She was perched to enjoy all that straight-privileged life had to offer, and the least they could do, was get Julia where she was headed without being extra about it.

Road games. Julia yanked Polaroids from the van wall one-by-one at each mile marker, starting with the first one that she had tacked up. The timeline reflected a once happy, if bizarre, love triangle. She was stoned and on a fast track to tinnitus blasting Arthur Russell's *World of Echo*. The album was one of Franklin's cultural contributions to her life. "All-Boy, All-Girl" played as she progressed to the most recent Polaroids. The secret couple inside the throuple became, in a word, obvious. How had she missed what was right in front of her face? Angry with herself, she abandoned the travel game and pulled down all the remaining Polaroids into one hefty stack. They were her Polaroids after all. Let them stop her! She put them into the front compartment of her backpack and then crawled around the floor stuffing rogue belongings beneath the main zipper. She remembered that the Three of Swords reversed had medicine, and when she arrived at Franklin's she intended to hang like a bat and let the blades slide free.

* * *

The van stopped. Unabomber Julia wasn't sure how long they were parked in front of Franklin's house before she looked up. The driver and passenger stared at her as if behind the shades and hoodie was sixteen-year-old prodigy Ted Kaczynski, before the CIA ignited the problematic incel by dosing him with LSD. Her heart felt dead to them. Julia kicked an empty bag of Flamin' Hot Cheetos. Her stomach growled. The sound was honest and to the point. She was hungry, her animal body exiled from Meerkat Manor. Flower dead from a snake bite. In earlier times, Reggie would have enjoyed her stoney baloney line of flight.

Reggie opened the door and stood there, arms crossed. Julia teetered under her swollen backpack as she gathered up the rest of her belongings. She slid from the van for the last time. Reggie shut the door behind her then leaned against it with all her weight. She longed for Julia to invite her inside. She wanted to know what splendor lived behind Franklin's class jump. Julia was too high to process, and too hurt. It seemed like a bad idea to spend more time together. Best laid plans. She needed a clean break. She looked at Reggie, at her heartbreakingly sexy femme-stache, and said, "He named his van Vance. You should name your first baby Babette. Have a really great marriage. I look forward to ignoring your registry." Julia stomped off in her backpack, arms loaded with thrifted outerwear, while Reggie refused to feel bad about her life choices. Sure, she had chosen an unremarkable man. Soon enough Julia would forget his name and remember him only as Vance.

Reggie felt torn by Julia's stoicism. She climbed into the passenger seat and watched Julia with the door still ajar. If Julia turned back, Reggie would jump free and try for a different outcome. Julia made it to the porch and stopped short. Reggie's pulse quickened. Julia flipped her a bird without looking back. Reggie felt stung. Vance suspected she might make a break for it. He removed his foot from the brake so that the passenger door swung shut. Julia was relieved to hear the tires peel out because she had no clue where to find the housekey. The last thing she wanted was an audience or their help. Julia fought back her tears. She felt around the door frame, fingered ceramics on the front porch, and tossed the rubber welcome mat aside. She remembered there was a lengthy text thread from Franklin about his house. She scrolled past his thoughtful words, her aggressive emoji replies—knives, chains, a zipper mouthed-face. She was rude, an ungrateful bitch, stupid, definitely not enough and way too much. What was she doing again? The key! She scrolled until she found a photo of the rock with the door key taped beneath it. Success. She was a smart bitch, kind of rad, she was everything, and even kept her word! Here she was, busy house-sitting for Franklin.

Julia pushed the front door into a mountain of paper that cascaded down from an overstuffed mail slot. Once she entered, it was clear that her main responsibility, the houseplants, were in terrible shape. It was dark and dusty. She was exhausted. What difference would a few more hours of neglect make? Julia closed a partially open shade, waded through the body of mail, and stumbled to the couch. She curled into the fetal position under a plush throw. It was too hard to remain awake without thinking about her family. It had been a year since the last time Julia was in this house.

The joint funeral, their shared father and her mother. A car and camper accident near Big Sur. Bad luck and worse timing. A tire blown out from a puncture. Rainstorm, slick roads, soft shoulder, lost control—car and camper skid off the coast. Oil, mud, rocks, cliff, sky, ocean, metal. Books just purchased at the Henry Miller Library, pots, pans, clothes, bedding, broken Mason jars of bulk bin classics—trail mix, popcorn, nutritional yeast, granola, oats, dried mango, weed—then camping gear, Patagonia, Sketchers, Dockers, and parents, Leonard (eighty), Jane (fifty-three), swam with the fishes.

It was early evening when Julia stirred. She opened all the shades to a soft light that illuminated glittery dust twirling in the air, somewhere between gross and magical. Julia needed to freshen up the space. She pushed the mail into a mound away from the front door. This felt like a major improvement and enough for the moment. She turned on lamps and snooped around the living room. Franklin was an eclectic plant daddy with an appreciation for Victorian decor. He seemed like someone who went to estate sales and snagged any choice object that made him feel like an otherworldly time traveler. That said, Julia never understood collecting other people's old photographs, let alone framing them. Who the hell were these campy ancestors in gold leaf frames? Franklin's people did not hail from the Dust Bowl or a mink farm. What a weirdo. Their shared father was shut down and never talked about his relatives. Julia wondered if a childhood without the internet had created some kind of fantastical longing for kin, or maybe this was just a creative exercise that helped Franklin write. Julia had only stayed here once before. She asked about the wall art, and he offered to take her thrifting as a way to deflect. She wondered if she would be equally weird and evasive in a couple decades. Things certainly seemed to be headed that way.

At ten years old, Julia discovered Franklin's castoffs in a trash bag and hid them in her closet. His counterculture books, mixtapes, and ephemera intrigued her long before she grasped their significance. The stash had an aura. She blamed it for making her sexually adventurous, drug-curious, and the amount of gay she seemed to be. That trash bag had ballooned into a museum, and she was once again under the influence of its curator. Not only that, she was the rogue caretaker of said museum. She fantasized about a relationship with

Franklin since she was a mere tween. He was seventeen years older, long gone, and she was under the impression that he had cut ties forever. Julia only asked about him once. She learned his name, and that he was a writer, after their parent's death. Julia bought his two novels, devoured them, and idolized Franklin once more. He had real stories to tell and a life to draw from while Julia was still in the process of figuring herself out.

Their father was an old man. Julia's mother, Jane, met Leonard as his graduate student. It was an imbalanced affair that meant Julia was the material realization of Leonard's year-long indiscretion. Franklin lived with his mother during the separation and discovered her suicide before divorce papers were signed. Franklin would not get the settlement items his mother had intended for his future. Leonard rejected him for being queer and trans, the trans part came later, but was clearly also a problem. There was no funeral for Franklin's mother because of Leonard's shame and unwillingness to put his young bride-to-be and newborn in the exacting crosshairs of colleagues, family and friends. Franklin was heartbroken over his mother's death and cried often.

Leonard decided that Franklin was a morose cloud who was old enough to exist in the world elsewhere. Julia did not know specifics. She was just a baby and had no memories of that time, just a garbage bag secret treasure trove and a journal with some of Franklin's wry descriptions. Franklin always had the gift of words. His mother did not sound like a pleasure cruise, and she definitely had serious mental health issues. Leonard gave up on her, upgraded to an easier life with tenure and a hot young wife. It was a second chance, better off without reminders of the first failure. Franklin was seen as a bad influence and just plain weird. There were times when he reminded Leonard of his dead ex-wife. Leonard preferred to think only of his young new family. Kicked out, iced out, or left on his own, the journal did not say, so it was never clear to Julia. Jane was only eleven years older than Franklin, first she avoided him as a person, then later the subject of him altogether. She only mentioned Franklin once, when Julia brought her first girlfriend home and Leonard went on a tear about his deviant children. There were no family pictures with Franklin. His author photos did not ring a bell. Without the accident, their paths may have never crossed.

Julia grew tired from familial reflection and plopped onto the couch. An envelope with her name handwritten in black ink rested against a ceramic paperweight that looked like one of those yellow plastic evidence numbers. Who buys something grim like that? She wanted one. Julia unfolded the brief note, nothing written that he hadn't already texted, except that he restated his generous offer. Free rent in exchange for taking care of his plants and applying to art school. He even offered to pay the entry fees to anywhere she applied, if that felt like an obstacle. She glanced at the dead and dying houseplants. Julia was the obstacle. He would have to offer her some latitude because of her recent breakup. Right?

A book on the coffee table caught her eye. It was a survey of the work of fine art photographer Evil Fated. A self-portrait in her younger leather dyke days graced its cover, shaved head, piercings, a fully tattooed bull dagger that made Julia's heart race. She pulled the thick hardback towards her and placed her finger on Evil's lips. Swoon! Why was Julia born too late? She imagined herself just outside of the frame of this photo in Evil's studio, wearing a pair of men's white briefs, yanking the cap off a beer bottle with her teeth. She would have spat the cap on the floor then handed the cold beer to Evil after she snapped the now iconic self-portrait. Evil would have said, "Thanks babe." Julia heard a cough.

She jumped and wielded the book as protection. Another cough, a clear-as-day cough that made her crawl behind the couch to cower. The coughs grew pathetic. Julia crawled around to find the source. A fern. A near-dead fern coughed, and she could hear it. That was not actually possible. Was she asleep? No.

"Water," the plant cried out.

"Please … water … I'm dying here," followed by more coughs.

Julia ran to the kitchen to get a glass of water then ran back and dumped it on the fern.

"Drowning … help … I'm drowning."

Julia ran at full speed into the bathroom and shut the door behind her. The clawfoot bathtub was irresistible so she turned on the hot water. She just needed to relax. Clearly, hearing the plants talk to her was some kind of stress response, only a minor psychological break. Heartbreak could do that. The stress of needing to apply to school and all those thoughts about her family's past. Her parents' untimely death! She undressed as the hot water ran and pushed down on the plug at the bottom of the tub. She stared into the mirror as it fogged and obscured her face.

A sad hanging plant behind the door sang "Take a Look at Me Now" like a wilted Phil Collins. Julia grabbed it from the hook. As she crossed the living room with the dying plant, other plants yelled that she was a murderer. Sounds came from every room. "Murderer … murderer!" Julia screamed back, "It was plantslaughter. Accidental! A misunderstanding. I'm sorry!" She was pissed. She hated being yelled at.

Julia found a robe and threw it on. She performed the arduous task of putting every single dead and dying houseplant out on the front porch. There were so many of them. Franklin had too many plants. It was absurd. Just get a dog. The coughing, crying houseplants were endless. Even the succulents had a kind of twee whine that made her feel batshit bananas. She did a final pass and noticed a wilted Swiss cheese plant crying out for its mother. She ran it outside and scanned for similar leaves. The dying plants continued to call her a murderer. She yelled, "Fuck you, Little Shop of Horrors, fuck you!"

Sensing a strangely penetrative vibe, Julia felt someone looking at her and noticed a man on the sidewalk. She closed her robe, ran back inside, locked the door, and returned to the bathroom. She nearly scalded her finger in the bathwater. She returned to the living room and retrieved the coffee table book with the hot bull dagger artist on its cover. She closed the bathroom door. She placed her robe on the closed toilet seat and sat on it. She leaned the book against the wall so she could admire the hot leather dyke. Julia masturbated for the cover butch and periodically tested the bathwater temperature without breaking character. It was incredibly hot. The water and her rich fantasy life. She stopped short of saying Evil's name but stared into her eyes so intensely that it almost felt real.

2

Avery stood on the sidewalk and self-berated. He had a plump semi from the beautiful stranger's open robe and a spank-bank deposit slip penned by his brain, the sight of her emblazoned with precision down to the shape of her nipples. He would feel bad calling it forth when he got home later, and the dread would turn him on even more. Disgusted with himself for being such a basic man, he gathered his book-filled tote onto his shoulder and dashed across the street. That he was wearing his "I'm With Her" Aileen Wuornos t-shirt today made matters worse. Everything pointed back to the reason the white cis-het-man had lost enrollment in his Women's Studies classes. Regardless of his fierce dyke mother and the world he was raised in, Avery was a stupid boy. His ex-girlfriend promised that she too had a Criterion Collection of masturbatory material hoarded from real world encounters. She said he was healthy and human. He felt there was a power differential between them that made her erotic curation unimpeachable. For him, it was just gross. He knew at least that much from reading underrated and amazing lesbian literature.

His nameless ex was a full professor and one of only two tenured women in the philosophy department. During Avery's second semester adjunct teaching on campus, the two were seated next to each other at a conference. She approved of Avery's notes, plucked the pen from his fingers, and scribbled her number in the margin. She was tired of dating a certain kind of asshole. Avery was unfamiliar. He read for pleasure and enjoyed penetration. He was a rebound she loved objectively more than subjectively, but she moved him into her apartment anyway. Bountiful intrigue and adventure ensued for a time before she slid into the backwaters of unresolved trauma. She was wildly self-sufficient but deeply straight. Prior to Avery she was solely drawn to men she could be mean to but also fear. Avery sought a kind of intimacy that felt like a trap. She fantasized about cheating on him and voiced her designs during pillow talk to poke holes in his tightening sheath. He thought it was a flirtatious game, outlandish and humiliating in a way that he enjoyed.

With Avery's lack of employment, her subtle need for an escape hatch took center stage. He was always around. She began to share whatever was on her mind in real time. The night they broke up she returned with take-out from their favorite Mediterranean spot. She was aglow from her brief exchange with the hot falafel guy and overshared that he was a regular in her fantasy exploits. Sometimes her fantasies included customers who had to wait in line while they had sex next to the register. Avery asked if she ever thought about the falafel guy when they were intimate. "How can I? You consistently interrupt my inner life with a cloying need for me to be present when we fuck." He assumed she was joking, a bit more acerbic than her usual wit, but still. He loved her and thought they would be married someday.

Avery lifted the oily paper bag from the coffee table and darted to the kitchen. He threw on an apron and dropped his jeans.

Flustered, she stopped him. She didn't feel that Avery could success-fully perform the role of a hard-working, short, stocky, olive-skinned man in a tight red skullcap in a way that wouldn't ruin it for her forever. Avery saw that she was serious. A sick feeling washed over him akin to when he received the job loss email. Just as suddenly, his relationship was yanked from beneath his feet so fast he had whiplash. Their conversation grew unwieldy. It began with a dis-course on courage, desire, mental snapshots of butt cracks and cleavage, followed by her impromptu keynote address in which Avery was summarily asked to move out because he lacked a certain je ne sais quoi. She wanted to masturbate in peace and told him to sleep on the couch until he figured something else out. The buzz of her highspeed wand reverberated from the bedroom. Avery was a single, out-of-work academic in an area of study that had moved on without him.

* * *

The gothic charm of his mother's home failed to warm the chill that coursed through his body at the prospect of returning to the nest. He was in his early forties and his mid-life crisis did not match the stereotypically fun propaganda. He lacked a new sports car and date half his age. The house was dark, save the light in his mother and her girlfriend's bedroom. His boner was gone and so was his tor-ment around self-pleasure and self-recrimination. He hurried into the guest room and clunked his tote onto the ridiculously petite writing desk. His suitcase was wedged in the corner, and he was definitely living out of it.

Joggers, hoodie, and slides, then off to the kitchen he went. Avery was unsure what to eat. He didn't feel like cooking and forgot to go shopping. He was already eating their groceries, which broke one of the rules he'd devised in order to maintain his adult independence, so he checked the cabinets for something small and unnoticeable. A sack of cookies called out. He tried one and it was delicious. Alright, Santa. He grabbed a dessert plate and placed a healthy stack in its center, got a glass of milk.

As Avery made his way down the hall, he couldn't help but eavesdrop as his name rang out. He heard Catherine, his mother's girlfriend, who was closer to his age than hers, make fun of him for teaching Women's Studies. She said something sarcastic, but he didn't catch the entirety of her thought, just the horror of his mother's response: "Avery is not some incel who never left my basement. He just got dumped and had to move. And then he learned that there wasn't enough enrollment for his classes. As an adjunct, that's it. Semester employment gone. It isn't like he earned enough to have any savings. Please be nice." Catherine apologized but voiced her concerns about a grown ass man living in their space. Avery silently pushed back—it was his mother's house. Who was Catherine to question his presence? Like he was some little boy crying for his mommy's help? Avery went pale at the sight of his cookies and milk. He slunk back to the kitchen. He poured the milk down the drain and put the cookies back in their sack. He was a grown ass man. He put on running shoes to take a walk.

Avery wondered if he should go to the food store. He needed to do things that would help him keep a shred of dignity. He would go to the barber soon, and he would continue to do his own laundry. He had to figure out what was next, forget that he ever earned a doctorate or taught at a college level. What were his interests? Who was he beyond the realization of a dyke community project to create a soft-masculine prince able to run a Food Not Bombs kitchen for ten years without hitting on a single female volunteer? Avery wanted to break free. This was about him as a soul with a purpose that could exist in full now that his mother's dreams for him were sated. It was actually a gift that he couldn't teach Women's Studies anymore. He was going to get in touch with his true ambition and life goals. Maybe he would get a job at a falafel place and wear a skullcap to work. He could be a willing subject to the female gaze. He sure as hell was always going to be on every lease from now on and also would never move in with anyone again. His future girlfriends and wives would have to cohabitate under *his* roof. He would never get kicked out again. Just as soon as he figured out his new path and had an income, watch out world. Avery understood that this was his mid-life crisis. The stereotypical trappings were smoke and mirrors. He must have been going the wrong way and this was the necessary course correction. It was so unfortunate and embarrassing.

His mind needed a distraction, music or a podcast, anything but his own thoughts. He pulled out his phone and a reflection caught his eye in the black glass. A blinking light, or was it more of an orb? Avery pocketed his phone as he looked up at the sky. Six orbs total doing some kind of geometric peacocking. They drifted into two triangle shapes that fanned out and then looped in a circle. Could be military, or a private fleet—some kind of joke? There was something, well, out-of-this-world about them. Their speed and transformation, visible and invisible, the eerie silence too. Something was happening. Whatever it was, Avery had a sense that it had to do with him. It was wildly egotistical to think such thoughts. People don't just get a private UFO demonstration out of nowhere, but no one else was around. He didn't see any neighbors in any windows. He was all alone, and the orbs knew it.

Finally, headlights approached. Avery raced up to the car and waved at the driver through the windshield. The driver kind of clocked him as he pointed up at the sky. The driver did not want to be involved and sped off. Avery felt like it was the driver's loss, but he remained anxious for another witness. Lone UFO sightings make people seem bananas. He was still all alone when the orbs disbanded. His heart sank. The orbs deserved his full attention but instead he had focused on finding someone to share the experience with, a secondary witness. Avery watched the skies above. *Please come back*, he beamed to the UFOs with every fiber of his being. And with that, they did. Whether it was coincidental or not, it would be of greater consequence in the near future.

Avery reached a roundabout with a cracked foundation strewn with used nitrous canisters. He ran to its center and the orbs circled overhead. What happened next was the hardest part to share and would have to remain secret for a time. Avery felt the connection between them, it was like static cling and he was a sock pressed against an invisible fabric drawing him in by his body hair alone. The hair on his head, his little chest hairs, arm hairs, leg hairs, even his pubes were at full attention poking into his underwear. Through this connective electric field, Avery asked the ships to form a rectangle while picturing a rectangle in his mind's eye. The orbs obliged.

He raised his arm and pointed to the left, they went left. Same for right. He made and released fists then imagined them blinking. The orbs blinked their lights on and off at least three times. He lost count. He was too busy clenching his bowels so he didn't poop himself in the street. It was a bit much for his mental state. The ships twirled and sped off. Avery was unsure if he just told them he needed to go take a shit, that he was too mentally unstable to receive their message. He regretted asking for proof by making them be circus orbs, like he was the UFO ringmaster. His heart rang out. *Please come back and take me with you!!! I'm sorry.*

He felt his insides twist. It was a feeling worse than heartbreak or being fired. He started to collapse onto the cement but again he felt like a sock in a dryer. His arm hair stood tall. He looked at the sky and a single orb zipped left, right, blinked or more likely winked, at him. It disappeared. The message was clear. Avery was not alone, and had at least one new orb friend, possibly six.

Avery needed to go to the bathroom. It was unlikely that he could make it back to the house in time. He wasn't near an alley with a dumpster to duck behind. This was suburban sprawl with landscaping galore. Avery noticed a woman walking her dog up the block. He tried to stay well-lit in the street to flag her down in the most non-threatening fashion he could muster. He asked her for an extra doggy waste bag. Together they eyed the fat roll attached to her leash. She would have been a horrible person to deny him. She handed him a thin green wad of plastic and, using only her eyes, asked where his off-leash dog was.

"Thank you! Dreaded double poo!" he called, not looking back.

Avery found a dark corner to slip between neighboring hedges. He released all judgement and took a crap on someone's yard. He was quick and self-contained about it. It looked like an oversized candy bar, and he was able to get it into the bag without incident. He tossed it into a someone's trash can on the way home and soon forgot about it. It was definitely the least interesting part of the night. He looked forward to wiping himself, but there were bigger fish to fry. He had interacted with intelligent life from another planet.

The light was still on in his mother's bedroom when he returned. He decided to shower and calm down. It was impossible not to wonder what his mother and Catherine were saying about him now. He inhaled and stepped into the warm shower. He exhaled, and in that moment realized his life had taken the kind of unexpected turn one might only happen upon in queer literature—a dyke mom, a UFO, a scandalized neighbor who did not deserve an explanation.

3

Seated in bed with her legs extended, Evil Fated entered grades into her laptop underneath a life-size self-portrait from the '90s. She justified its location to all who inquired by noting that if she were Robert Mapplethorpe, she would have had an equally large print of *Self Portrait With Whip* above her bed. She loved that image. Robert's eyes burned through the lens. His perfect ass checks clenched around the whip's handle, subjugating the viewer. Evil's self-portrait was equally on fire, but for now her work only went so far. That said, she knew the parade of women she brought home, both in and out of sobriety, imagined themselves in bed with the younger Evil. Her current partner, Catherine, once caught Evil looking lustily at herself while they had sex. Evil denied it but it was true. Her bed was an altar that required feeding and all the little deaths that transpired there were sacrifices to the god of her former self and the demons she wrestled—lest anyone forget. The young ones never noticed her biggest faults. She kept it casual and heated. But Catherine, a woman in her fifties, who would continue to be fierce and gorgeous for many decades to come, had changed everything. She helped keep Evil's reckless side at bay. The challenge was simply to keep pace with Catherine. It wasn't just that she could cut Evil down to size. Catherine could julienne her ego and plate an entire charcuterie board in one look. Evil did everything to avoid that look, which also helped her stay present.

Catherine smoked an herbal cigarette and blasted through emails. She repositioned herself on the pillow to make her chest more prominent but pretended to be totally immersed in her work. She waited for Evil's hand to menace her upper thigh, but it remained on the keyboard. Catherine's mind spiraled back to Avery's arrival. She grew so distracted that the fractals on her screensaver mirrored her inner world. Each fractal blob echoed that Avery's arrival had ended their active sex life. It was the end of walking around naked. Catherine wanted to throw a tantrum but could not. She imagined writing an AITA letter but couldn't shake the feeling that she *was* the asshole. She was. She did not want to be like her mother, forever unsatisfied. She did not want to make doves cry. That said, a grown ass man, closer to her own age than her partner, was now in her daily life. She regretted giving up her own place and moving in with Evil. She loved that Evil was a good parent. Someone who was kind enough to say yes when her son was in need. But why was an adult straight cis white man in his forties having to move in with his mother and her girlfriend? He was *also* the asshole for asking. The real problem was not knowing how long this arrangement would last. If she knew the end date, then she would not be unraveling.

She pretended to review a contract, refusing to silently come apart next to her lover. Catherine's career had finally taken off and her travel schedule made time at home even more precious. She was out of town when this had unfolded without a hitch, without a question about his trajectory. Avery was a problem. Catherine had to say something. So she did.

Evil declined to ask her son to pin down an exit date. She was not willing to make him feel unwelcome in her home, to demand a timeline. He would stay as long as he needed. The conversation made Catherine feel terrible in a way that felt unhealthy. They were happy before he moved in. Catherine was not one to sit on her hands. She tossed her tablet onto her nightstand and lowered to the floor. She began an explorative search into their under-the-bed storage. She located the bin with the lesser used sex toys and retrieved a ball gag. Then she found some soft rope. Massage oils were useless, as were feathers and other bullshit that seemed romantic the first month they had dated. She tossed those back into the bin. Catherine curated a pile of toys like a prepper making an emergency go-bag to forestall the disastrous end of their sex life. Evil sensed an erotic shift in her immediate surroundings and rolled over to see what all the fuss was about. She was a beat too late. Catherine held a very promising fistful of dildos but was fixated on a picture of gorgeous young thing from Evil's past.

"I didn't know that was in there," Evil grimaced. It was inarguably terrible form to have a photograph of an ex amidst shared sex toys. Catherine was torn between the fact that the photograph was both a work of Evil's art that should be properly archived, and simultaneously, Evil's ex cohabitating with their intimates. If dicks weren't both costly and personal, she would have made an impromptu fire pit in the bathroom sink. It was cathartic to imagine. Catherine was stuck on the bounds of what needed archiving and what belonged in the trash or inside her body ever again, an awkward quagmire that brought displeasure. She didn't want to deal with it but was grateful to be annoyed about something other than Avery. It was a solid substitute. She left the mess on the floor, grabbed her cigarettes, and fled to the kitchen to think. Evil should and would be left to deal with the ex in the box.

Evil rolled back to her side of the bed and hid behind her laptop until the coast cleared. It could have been worse. The ex could have been wearing the very same ball gag in the photograph. *Was* it the same one? Evil felt like a real cheapskate and decided *that* was the high crime that sent Catherine on her way. Catherine deserved her own toy box. Evil had money. What the hell was wrong with her? She put the ball gag in the trash along with most items, save for a few dicks that felt like old friends she was eager to return to her repertoire.

Evil grabbed her laptop. She held her breath as she typed, afraid that her favorite San Francisco sex shop would be shuttered. The online store appeared, and she was in business, racing through virtual aisles, improving her lot with a new ball gag, flogger, paddle, arty Jackson Pollock splatter-painted dildo from Scandinavian designers, metal butt plug shaped like a motorcycle and replacement nipple clamps. She began to obsess over a new harness, but she owned a superior collection. Some things were timeless. No need for new leather adornments from the sex store. She grabbed a few candles, being a sucker for hot wax. Some organic lube and a vibrator that she could sync to her phone for long distance play. Not that she ever would even figure out how to use such a thing, but the various scenarios to employ the device were titillating. She placed the order.

When she saw Catherine next, her first words were "Don't worry babe, I fucking fixed it." Catherine was unsure what she meant, but always cherished a sense of repair.

4

Julia stood at Franklin's kitchen table and stared at her spiral note-book. She was spiraling too. She wrote the word "portfolio" in black marker. She wrote the word "Polaroids" in pen, numbered "1." on a ten-point bullet list. Only nine more work samples to go. She would have to create new work just to know what else to put on the list. She needed to clear her mind and opened the refrigerator to remove rotten produce. Her energy needed to transform, more creative climbs, away from death. The rot wasn't as bad as she thought it would be. Franklin was considerate to stock the fridge but didn't go overboard. She collected wilted kale, stinky sloshy spinach, and limp carrots the texture of ear plugs. It gave her the idea to make carrot-shaped ear plugs with long green tops that would be practical but also fun, little earrings for a loud concert or for use at bedtime. It would give her a real thrill to pluck a carrot out of an ear. If she sculpted a pair and called it a sculpture, would that count as a second portfolio item? The carrot should signify something, should act as a stand in for something meaningful to her or society at large. Carrot ear plugs should communicate an idea, a concept or stake a philosophical claim. Instead, the sculpture fell flat, a joke gift from

Spencer's. It was a stupid idea and so upsettingly capitalist and meaningless that she shut her notebook in between emptying cartons of milk and OJ.

What a waste. It was presumptuous to buy dairy milk. Had Franklin even consulted her on what groceries she might like? Was the act of gifting groceries so heroic that it outweighed a simple check-in? She felt sad for the cow. Then mad at Franklin. She scrolled back through her texts until she saw his inquiry into her diet restrictions. She had sent him a middle finger in response. She was the problem. Why was it so hard to text him back using words? It was worse that he was so understanding. She wondered if it was because he was a trans man. Like, maybe he totally understood that sometimes you don't want to respond to some man's questions about diet, or anything else. He seemed to have a real handle on misogyny and patriarchy and had his own Axe deodorant to grind.

Julia did not know Franklin well. The death of their shared father and her mother had drawn them into this strange web of care, care that Franklin never received but wanted to offer Julia. Julia did not know how to receive anything that lacked a transactional ring to it. She was half-raised by the same parent who fucked up Franklin. She had trust issues. Watching Franklin's house rent-free in exchange for her to apply to school was a sleight of hand. Franklin was not really getting anything back. Not even living houseplants. She was in his house rent-free, not honoring their agreement, and he was in another country. What would he do? Rent out his house from afar? Was there some friend in the wings ready to physically remove her from the premises for breach of agreement? Would he call the cops? No. He would never call the cops. Some of the books baby Julia inherited from him were abolitionist primers like *Angela Davis: An Autobiography* and *Soledad Brother: The Prison Letters of George Jackson*. Julia wasn't sure if he had any friends in town. His social media presence was author-related. All of his photographs were thrifted acquisitions. Who was this guy? Regardless, she could easily lie about everything and get him new plants. She could lie about getting rejected from school. There were many ways to handle the situation without keeping her end of the deal. She could apply to school and overcome her warped feelings about not deserving his care. She could do what she said she would do, aside from care for the houseplants she had already killed. Too late for that. The school application deadline was fast approaching.

Julia gathered up the trash and compost. She hopped over the dead houseplants arranged in sad rows on the porch. As she landed, she heard one of them sigh, "… dignified burial." *Motherfucker*, she thought as she darted around the side of the house to dump the bags in respective bins. She plugged her ears on her way back but swore she could still sense the plant mouthing the words *dignified burial*.

Safely out of plant earshot, she went to the bedroom. She grabbed her phone. The last text from Franklin was a cat video, a tuxedo cat's face and paws photoshopped over Marlene Dietrich in the classic film *Morocco*. Franklin was an objectively hot transmasc novelist at large. Why was he texting her cat videos all the time? She couldn't remember if that had something to do with the book he was writing, but that felt vaguely correct. She wondered if she would ever get to travel to Morocco or ever leave the west coast. Her brain recoiled in anguish over her newly lost van life throuplehood adventures. A man with a plan and a van, what more did a couple of lesbos need? They should have just gotten their own damn van. Julia missed Reggie and also hated Reggie. She refocused on the cat video to garner whatever light drop of dopamine was on furry offer. Julia composed a response to Franklin. "I killed your plants but your house is fine." Then she deleted it. She hearted his video instead, high praise coming from her, and then she closed with a single water gun emoji. The usual shame spiral that came with texting Franklin never arrived because she was at his house, rather than faking it to make it.

She opened a browser and typed "dignified burial for plants." Sites about green burials, bio urns, and burial pods appeared. She was impressed that the dead plant on the front porch knew a little something about its funerary wishes. Nature was wild. Julia selected a link at random and sadly learned that these burials were intended for humans. She failed the dying plants again. But she was resourceful and creative. It took less than a minute to decide that, with a shovel and a hole, she could be the provider of a green burial. It would conveniently eliminate all evidence of her house-sitter shortcomings. She would have put the plants in the green bin for the city to compost and never have given it another thought. Now, she could hardly consider a more undignified burial than dumping them into a black trash bin with actual garbage.

Julia dug a smaller hole than the one she imagined she would dig. She did not love digging and wanted the task to be over from the moment she hoisted the first pile of dirt. But it looked deep and wide enough to be a houseplant grave. Julia made her way to the porch and back full of apologies. With each plant she repeated, "I am very sorry. I am returning you to the earth. I hope your future is brighter than this. I hope you feel elevated to at least the status of a beloved family pet."

Julia returned with the final plant. There was something about the ritual nature of the back-and-forth that sparked a need for an additional body. She ran inside to the kitchen and grabbed a few of the Polaroids she had taken of Reggie and Vance. She situated the Polaroids underneath some yellow and dark brown vines.

"I apologize to all of you. It was because of my choices and behaviors that you have all died, for real or figuratively. I should have held my boundaries and trusted my instincts. You would be alive, and I would be here with Reggie. We would have watered you regularly and made sure you had enough light. Okay, that is probably not true. You would have been watered sometimes and as far as light and care, a lot would have remained desired, but you would be alive. I would still be in a relationship. But the world doesn't work that way, and sometimes there are hard lessons. I did not give Reggie an ultimatum because I was scared she would choose Vance. I did not want to hear her say it, and I was unable to trust her. Little Orpheus had to turn around. If I had been chill and just let her sleep with him for a bit, well, you would all still be dead, but I might have a relationship. But, like, why would I *want* that relationship? He was stupid. Right? Should I have said nothing once I knew their deal? Just went with the flow while Reggie and Vance hooked up behind my back? Trust that it would burn out, and eventually she would wonder what she was thinking? But then she would have lied to me, and *that* would have been a whole thing. Feelings are stupid. I am getting off track. The point is, Reggie is the real reason you are dead. For she is the true murderer! She killed love. She made me kill you. I should have done a better job with my boundaries or whatever, that could have changed the course of things. But it was her fault, and really, Vance was the one who should have just respected that we were in a monogamous relationship. He did not have to pursue anything with us. He could have had one wild night with two homos and dropped us off. Why the cross country throuple act when clearly it was Reggie or bust?

I hereby bury Vance and Reggie and throuplehood. These Polaroids signify the composting of all of my mistakes. My regrets and apologies to you my plant friends. I will think of you when I pick out your replacements and tell them you were their plantcestors. I hope this is a dignified burial. I hope being returned to the earth feels right and good. Like maybe you are just changing forms and mixing things up. I don't know, maybe like Reggie, you felt trapped. Maybe it sucks to be a houseplant. Maybe it sucks to be domesticated or held captive in some strange place. I have no idea if Franklin was a good plant parent or super annoying. I ruined everything but also maybe not. I hope you are happy that you get to move on to whatever the next great beyond will mean for you. I hope it is really cool, and that disintegrating into soil and banging into mycelium, roots, and other dead plants feels like a fun underground orgy. I hope it is like a big party where you get held up and honored for your time spent on this cruel and weird planet with toxic air. I hope that you are happy to transform in this yard, this place that you have been calling home for however long you have lived here. You were special and singular. I am sure you brought joy and life into Franklin's house. I hope he was way better to you. I was wrong and should have been here. I need to get better at that kind of stuff. You have been helpful in teaching me that. Your deaths are not in vain. Also, I buried my throuple here too. It returns to earth. We move on and change forms. We become something new."

Julia heard a brief snarky laugh. It was the hedge closest to the grave. Julia wanted to ignore the hedge but unfortunately had become too vulnerable during the burial.

"What is your problem?" Julia demanded.

The hedge hedged for a moment, then expressed its controversial position that indoor plants have it easy. They are overly dependent and too delicate. Julia did not disagree, but because of the hedge's tone, she took an adversarial stance.

"And lawn hedges are wild and free?"

The hedge laughed. She was not wrong. Julia did not know why this was happening to her. It was so next level that she asked the opinionated greenery, "Why is this happening to me?"

The hedge was more than ready and willing to answer. But Julia, feeling tired, decided she only meant it rhetorically and was no longer ready or willing to hear a reply. She ran back inside with her ears covered. She was untethered, unmoored, undone! She had convinced herself that the chlorophyll chatterboxes would be a thing of the past once the indoor plants were gone, something she would take to her own grave. Now it seemed far from over. She ran inside, "Damn it. Damn it. Damn it."

She pulled out her phone and texted Reggie. *Hey quick totally random question about trimming. Can there be a delayed high from THC exposure, like a hallucinogenic effect? Are you experiencing anything like that? Or nevermind, I don't know, you can disregard. Hope you are okay.*

She hit send and put the phone in her pocket. She was more than a little freaked out. She rushed over to Franklin's record player and lowered the needle onto the LP already on the turntable. Blondie, *Parallel Lines*. Her heart ached as soon as she heard the lyrics about an unanswered call. She jumped around the living room and gave herself over to Debbie Harry.

Her presence of mind returned once the song was over. Julia regretted that she did not burn the entire stack of Polaroids, but then she realized how deeply satisfying it would be to use their relationship to get into an art school. She could exploit the throuple with a thoughtful triptych. There were a number of photographers that she greatly admired who made work drawn from their lives. Nan Goldin for one, Evil Fated for two. She decided to review all of her Polaroids and her phone's photo album with a "work sample" approach.

5

Franklin's phone swished with the arrival of a water-gun emoji from Julia. The close-up of her face with a googly-eyed unibrow as her contact photo never failed to amuse. Franklin sipped from a bottle of bubbly water. He cracked his knuckles. His fingertips resting gently on the laptop keys *ASDF JKL;* as he glanced up at images tacked to the wall: famous artists and their cats, fictional character references for his novel in progress. Andy Warhol, Frida Kahlo, Patti Smith, Jean Cocteau, Jean-Michel Basquiat, Yoko Ono with their respective felines interspersed with Post-it notes and index cards. Among the familiar art stars were a less than famous duo Henry the influencer and his tuxedo cat, Edith.

Franklin was awarded the residency to work on his third novel. He refused to think of it as his junior work because the pressure of his last novel nearly killed him. He was simply writing a book. *Just Cats*, he thought as he regarded the spine of Smith's *Just Kids*. He decided to name the next chapter "cats, cats, cats, cats" because he was writing about his fictional Patti Smith character, Patti. And his novel was about cats not horses. Primarily it was about cats and masculinity. Patti was his favorite character. In real life, Smith's Scorpio Abyssinian cat was named Cairo. Franklin named Fictional Patti's cat "Vegas." He cut up interviews and selected texts from *Just Kids* about Patti and Robert Mapplethorpe's friendship as well as her cat Cairo. Then he recast Robert as a composite character, being both himself as well as Patti's cat. Robert was a Scorpio just like her cat, so it was smooth sailing. Franklin cut and pasted a quote that described Robert as romantic and poetic, then traded out the name *Robert* to note that *Vegas* was romantic and poetic. Franklin was uncertain if the style was going to work with the rest of the novel. The residency gave him time to play around a bit. It also afforded him cover to be a justified shut-in for the sake of literature rather than confronting the mild agoraphobia that accompanied being trans. That said, he still had the internet and a never-ending streamy relationship with prestige cable dramas. Franklin put on Smith's *Horses* to conjure a mood. Full body chills as Patti's voice dug nails into his chest and back. *Cats, cats, cats, cats, coming in all directions white, tabby, orange, fluffy …*

Franklin's mind retreated to his high school hallway, his bullies, his tortured youth, his avoidant half-sister, their dead father, and the poet Rimbaud. Patti is a Capricorn. She has timeless style. Every queer including Franklin loved Rimbaud and especially David Wojnarowicz. All the young, drug-dusted, dead-too-soon faggots were lovable. They were also marketable. Someone, many someones, bought up their work because a dead faggot artist' art was worth more than a living one's. Franklin recalled a series of prints, Rimbaud's head worn as a mask by Wojnarowicz's friends and then photographed by him. There was something there, something to use in his novel. In his next chapter he decided Patti would meet Henry. It would be happenstance. In line at a bodega to buy the same brand of cat food. Maybe they would place their cat food on the counter at the same time. The fact that it was the same brand could imbue some kind of meaning … but like Patti would get salmon, and Henry chicken. Somehow, they would wind up outside on the sidewalk sharing photos of their cats. Then Henry would show Patti some art he was making, and Patti would be into it. Their friendship cemented on cement, it would turn into an artistic collaboration, the two of them photographing their friends wearing cat masks of Edith and Vegas. Patti seemed more masculine than Henry. Franklin wanted to do something with that tension. Inspired, but too heady to let it fall on the page, he knew to step back when his writing became too intellectual. But he had struck close to an idea. It could fuel him for hours when the alchemy hit, but it needed to be coaxed.

Franklin showered, shaved, and jerked off in front of the mirror. He liked to pretend he was a cam trans and position himself accordingly until he finished, then thank his imaginary audience. He had to flee from the mirror quickly or he would get depressed that he didn't have the abs, pecs, and obliques of his dreams. He was sinewy and a little hairy. The hair was never where he wanted it. Once he finished this book, he would work with a trainer. It would be a reward. He needed to get to work. He put on joggers then returned to his desk.

Franklin checked his feed out of habit. He observed one rule. Whenever Henry posted a new video, Franklin had to create a fictional counterpart video in his manuscript. The last time Henry posted, Franklin swapped out the Marlene Dietrich tuxedo cat in *Morocco* for a calico Cate Blanchett cat in *Carol*, her furry paws on Rooney Mara's shoulder. Franklin checked to see if there were any new posts to help him get back into his flow, but there were not. It was for the best since he needed to focus on the bodega scene with Patti. Currently, the skeleton key he employed to unlock writerly flow was sexual arousal and a bottle of Club-Mate. He opened a bottle of the latter and set a timer for five minutes. He opened a hookup app and cruised. After the timer ended, he would force himself to write regardless of his state.

6

Avery quickly searched the garage for camping gear. It was hard to dig through storage under pressure. He snagged a small lantern and a red sleeping bag with lightning speed from a black bin. His ears were trained to the sky just outside the open door. He knew there were tarps, mats, and a tent within reach but had trouble locating them. He had no clue when Evil had last camped. All the tubs were opaque and without labels. His quick search failed to yield anything outdoor related. He dreaded the thought of missing the orbs on another fly-by, and the weather was fine, so he abandoned the stab at additional comfort. He slowly shut the garage door behind him with a quiet grip.

Supine in the backyard, Avery kicked pants from his ankles and threw them like a ball onto the grass. He rolled his body into the sleeping bag and set his phone on his chest. He fixated on lights in the sky, was unclear if they were stars or corporate satellites. Avery needed a phone app to distinguish between them—the ouroboros gagged on its own tail. Life had ended, and the world only appeared to harbor people in motion like a long dead galaxy that was still visible lightyears away. The fact that Avery was a domino in a waterfall of pushy predecessors did not make him less accountable. He tried to be the best domino he could be. If intelligent life from another planet proved to be a stopgap or give rise to alternatives, Avery was all in. Unfortunately, he only had one encounter. He was too horny for the little green men to return. He was antsy, and wished he could call his ex to tell her about the orbs. That was a bad idea. She would seriously worry about his mental state in a way that he didn't want to ponder. Surely, he was in his right mind and had renewed life purpose, that part felt clear. If anything, he would be sharing good news. Everything had worked out for the better. Since she ended things, he had evolved in a personal growth spurt so profound that UFOs came calling. He did not need romantic companionship. No dating app offered SWM4ET for real.

His thoughts turned to anal probes then back to his ex. She would never finger his asshole again. Criminal. He clenched his tight hairy hole and imagined her slender wet digit. He felt robbed by the universe, but also liberated towards intergalactic relations. Alien anal probes might be butt play too bold for most straight men to cop to enjoying. Even straight women seemed angry about being abducted and anally probed. Most discourse made it sound like if you were taken, then you were destined to be a non-consenting human lab rat. People with crop circles were probably not PFLAG members or part of the BDSM community. Avery wondered about trans people and why they had no parents or friends. PFT ... LAG! He would have to share that observation with his mother in the morning. Her dark sense of humor was well earned. He probably shouldn't make that joke, had no right, but Evil would just think it was hilarious. He knew she and her friends would love it if he was gay. Throughout puberty and adolescence, he tried to get a boner over Tom of Finland drawings. He longed to become more interesting than some boring heterosexual guy. Avery couldn't change his nature and was one of the few people on the planet ready to respond to anyone who asked, *When did you know you were straight?*

Pre-slumber thoughts retreated, and the pang for his ex returned. Driven by hunger on autopilot, Avery opened his phone. He tortured himself with old photos of the two of them. She was rarely nice to him and extremely self-involved. She claimed to be broken like all of his girlfriends. Why should he judge anyone for coming apart under structural oppression, let alone rape culture? That said, he opened the album where he kept all the sexy selfies she had texted him over the years. He was immediately aroused and sorry for himself. He was broken too. He needed to delete all traces of her but was unable. He put an event called Fucking Delete It Dude in his calendar but kept changing the date. He would be mortified if she knew how hard it was for him. He lowered his phone and tried to sleep. He was uncertain, but his intuition told him that being asleep outside meant that the orbs could access him. Within that first exchange, he felt like he received a message that sleeping outside was important. It was hard to trust but equally hard to shake. Self-concern gnawed at his psyche.

Avery was tired yet wired. He returned to his phone and opened a porn site. An ad played at ten times the volume of anything else on the internet. He shut the site, waves of humiliation rippling across his body. He hid his phone and held his breath. A car backfired in the distance. Nothing else stirred and probably no one had heard the robotic moans. He lowered the volume and returned to the site. He scrolled through videos until he came across two women in a stairwell. One resembled his ex. He rolled onto his side, yanked his sock off with the other foot, then reached into the bottom of the bag to retrieve it. He drew the sleeping bag over his head and hit play. The beginning of the video was uninspired foreplay, so he closed his eyes and stroked himself to the audio. His fantasy played out alongside the porn's soundtrack. He imagined entering the stairwell. The women noticed him but pretended not to. They arranged their bodies so he had a better view, but they only did so because it brought them pleasure. He was their object. He waited until they beckoned him closer. The not-ex gestured for him to stop and lower his pants. She pointed at a step on the staircase above him. He sat down and rubbed his dick in his mind's eye as well as in the actual sleeping bag. Bored with his own horny limited imagination and ready for more visuals, Avery returned to the video. The actor who looked just liked his ex stared directly into the camera and licked her lips. The video cut to a lower angle where the not-ex ran her tongue across the ex lookalike's perineum. Avery felt jealous of the not-ex. He closed his eyes, traded places, and erased her from his new two-person scenario now he and the ex lookalike were in the porn stairwell. She yanked his hair to get him to hold still. Performative moans clipped in his phone speaker. It was confusing and hot. He finished in his sock inside of his mother's sleeping bag (regrettable). Heartbroken and sweaty, he realized that it was time to invest in some headphones.

Avery was almost ready to sleep but felt drawn to research recent UFO sightings. He learned that the acronym UAP, for Unidentified Anomalous Phenomena, was the newly preferred term. He typed a few key words into a search engine and a flood of video thumbnails appeared from around the world—New York, West London, Barcelona. Avery had no idea that people were trying to smoke on their balconies when orbs appeared in the sky. There was enough time and visibility for multiple cell phones to record the sightings. The orbs were different than his, but many also appeared in highspeed geometric arrangements. Some appeared during the day, others at night. The orbs lit up the sky in a particular shape and then shifted to another one, and all of this was documented by more than one witness. Plus, there were recent articles where the United States had admitted to UFO and UAP sightings and encounters. Documents had been released. It was such a sore subject, with so much judgement, both the scientific world and academia held a wide berth. ETs were like a drunk uncle that no one wanted to deal with. The area lacked legitimacy, even when there was hard evidence, unaltered videos, *proof,* it was still such a fringe topic. Avery's mind raced, but his body insisted on rest. He turned off his phone after viewing a video where a poet described seeing orbs around a lake in Seattle, every day, for weeks. Avery hoped his orbs would return to the roundabout, or more importantly, to him.

* * *

The kitchen window was soft with hazy morning light. Evil scooped beans into an aggressively loud grinder. She felt more tired than before she went to bed, which seemed unfair. She emptied grounds into the French press and glanced outside. She jumped at the appearance of a red sleeping bag in her backyard. She tightened her black silk robe and scanned the scene. First, she recognized her lantern, then balled up pants, and Avery's mop of hair. Her jaw loosened. She was wide awake from adrenaline and a coffee chaser.

Smoke spirals curled above two mugs. She set Avery's next to his foot since his hands were busy rolling up the sleeping bag. Evil pressed to see if there was something wrong with the guest room. She had never slept in there before. "Be honest."

Avery realized his cum filled sock was less than an inch from his mother. He grabbed it and shoved it in his balled-up pants but fumbled so the sock squished wetness into the denim. Avery wanted to will Evil away and shouted without meaning to, "It had nothing to do with the room!"

Evil's morning mind jumped headlong to the terrible prospect that he was having a breakdown. Avery collected himself quickly. He hid his clothes behind the sleeping bag, took up the coffee mug and stood facing her.

Evil studied his face, which had returned to its placid and steady demeanor.

Avery sipped coffee and mumbled "That is very good. Ethiopian?"

"No idea. Catherine buys it in eco-hip logo-free brown bags from some artisanal small batch specialty roast company near her gallery. I forget what the place is called."

Evil ground whatever was on the counter, without noting its hand scrawled origin. She could not taste hints of cherry or a burst of rose, and equally welcomed light, medium, or dark roasts. It was not her thing. So why was she in the backyard discussing potentially medium roasted Guatemalan coffee beans instead of Avery's decision to camp there? Evil was afraid to learn if it was her genetics at fault, or her parenting, or both. She inhaled an extra lung's worth of air then unleashed an express train of sentences to inquire if he was on drugs. Did he need fentanyl strips or meetings? Was this the reason why he had been broken up with and lost his classes? He could talk to her. No lack of recovery talk on tap.

Avery felt ashamed. He told his mother that addiction would have been a solid reason for his life coming apart as it had. Instead, it was more weather-related, like a shift in the gravitational field or magnetic pole reversals. He, a white cis hetero man, was not the person anyone wanted to learn Women's Studies from, and that was totally understandable. It was very cool for a time for him to be so invested in the field, but that moment had jumped the shark. His romantic relationship had also run its course. His ex desired someone to give her more psychic room than he ever could. He put it all together when she said that he crowded her, and she did not mean it literally. There must have been a too-thick, tangible quality to the way he loved. She wanted to be mysterious and unknown and free. He seemed lost, and that did not mix well with her aims. His aura was porous and had an odor that induced claustrophobia. Avery shared all of this with Evil in a slightly confused way over coffee. He apologized if he had brought the stink of being lost into her house, but he had good news. The stink should dissipate any time. He had a renewed life purpose. He did not want to talk about it, but wanted her to know, and he was totally sane. A road had opened.

Evil got what he was saying about his recent losses but was unable to connect any of that to him sleeping in her backyard. Avery stammered. He attempted to be vague, to suggest that a thing had happened, and his life would not be the same. It was not the kind of sentiment Evil could shrug off and then scramble up some eggs. Her look said as much. Avery revealed that he was scared of what she might think. She might question his sanity. He wondered what it would feel like to come clean. At least he could trust her.

Avery sounded matter of fact, "What is your experience was with close encounters of the fifth kind?"

Evil hummed the theme song from the movie about the third kind and punctuated it with a questioning *hmmm* at the end.

"No. Totally different. Fifth kind implies direct communication with UFOs."

Evil folded her arms, annoyed with the distinction. The mug in her fist warmed her bicep. She was suspicious of any UFO interaction that required him to sleep in her backyard rather than the guest room. The guest room was her least favorite room in the house. She was ready to lay blame there for most everything. Except UFOs. She cut to the chase.

"UFOs directed you to sleep in the yard? You know you can tell me anything?"

Avery shrugged. He was not prepared to field questions. Avery felt equal parts humiliated and unburdened as he told her the story. Six orbs were at large in her neighborhood, and he wanted to sleep outside in case they returned. He shared the full account but omitted the poop incident.

"Okay. Just don't tell Catherine."

"Tell me what?" Catherine asked as she approached from the kitchen. Evil did not expect her to be awake yet. She chugged the last of her coffee to buy time. Catherine's wild morning hair shot in all directions. She took a drag from a cigarette.

Evil chose to redirect. "When did you become a morning smoker?"

"You must have missed my newsletter."

Evil looked disappointed.

Catherine was annoyed, "They are only herbal cigarettes, lavender and skullcap! They calm me down!"

Evil smirked.

Catherine disappeared around the side of the house. Avery felt a weird tension between them. Something he never noticed before.

He asked if it was bad that he was there. Evil reassured him that no, he was not the problem, and he should stay as long as he wanted. No end date. He should feel comfortable to rest as long as he needed. Avery took that to mean that she thought he was crazy and an embarrassment. Worst of all, she did not believe that he was a UFO Contactee. He asked her point blank, "Do you believe me?"

Evil's mind darted to the *X-Files* then Gillian Anderson, how hot she was, definitely her type. Evil smiled at her son, "I want to believe!"

Avery nodded. He looked sad. Evil was too scared to ask if he was going to remain in the yard for the rest of the day. She did not want to know. She needed to shower and forget the past ten minutes. She returned to the kitchen and topped off her coffee with the tiny bit left in the press. She contemplated making a second pot but decided not to push her nerves into overdrive, lest she require her own herbal cigarette to calm down.

* * *

The shower was running when she entered the bedroom. Evil called out to see if she could join Catherine. Catherine did not hear her because she was too busy blowing smoke directly into the bathroom fan. Evil knocked and surprised Catherine, who extinguished her cigarette by plunging her hand into the shower. The wet herbs swirled to the drain like tea leaves, the soggy cigarette paper limp in her fingers. Feeling caught, she eagerly shared her morning shower. She opened the door, "Of course baby, whatever you want."

Catherine stepped into the water and used her toe to nudge the stubborn herbs down the drain. She washed her hair with conditioner. She rinsed it out as Evil ran the second shower head, then lowered to her knees and washed Catherine's well-manicured feet. It was unexpected, as was the subsequent lick up the length of her entire body. Evil used the additional shower head as a vibe on Catherine while gnawing on her neck and kissing her. Catherine had no clue what had gotten into Evil but was not mad about it. Evil needed somewhere to throw her entire being. She needed an emergency exit, and Catherine's body was her favorite place to visit. Catherine came fast and then mentioned the drought. Evil was disappointed, but shower sex first thing in the morning was far afield. She was also relieved not to have to deal with any questions about the backyard situation. Catherine made the effort to clarify she was into it but needed to get to work and could not take it to the bed, much as it pained her not to.

Evil remained under the hot water and used the second shower head to treat herself. Her mind was blank. She let the hot water run a beat longer and then did a cold plunge. She felt exactly like an icicle, albeit conscious and alert. Evil wrapped the towel around her waist and stood before the fogged mirror. She ran pomade through her black hair. She was curious about all the new products that had multiplied like Gremlins around the sink. Evil stole some moisturizer. She noticed a spot in the decoupaged magazine pin-up wallpaper she had created that was peeling off. A luscious leg kicked out and curled at the stiletto. Evil had an organic excuse to rummage around the garage to track down glue. She could "by chance" retrieve some items to help Avery with his camping needs, but not meddle in his affairs. She threw her Kenneth Anger *Lucifer* jacket over a black shirt and killed the lights.

7

Henry moved too quickly as he added a light to the top of his book-case. The clamp missed the shelf and the lamp dropped to the floor. Henry gasped. Edith was startled. She jumped to attention on the blue screen mat. Her furry tuxedo face grimaced. She stretched and gave Henry the once over with her bright green eyes. Henry was a vision in his teal romper and ankle socks. Edith was decisive with her energy expenditure and dramatic in general. It made her a movie star, Henry was sure about that. So sure, that he invested in head-shots with his foot long muse.

Edith made her way to the sunny spot by the window. Henry agreed to give Edith a twenty minute break. He could fuss with the setup in the meantime. His three point lighting was created from various yard sale lamps. He used additional lights to separate out the blue screen. He mounted his phone using a bendy tripod that he got from the dollar store. He kicked a box of props into the kitchen. His effort took over his entire studio apartment, but he was able to monetize his videos by allowing ads. Henry wanted to be a gay, Black, Jackson Galaxy-type figure, down to his own line of cat toys. His feline partner Edith was anti-work and had less of an interest in the finer things. Despite being only nine pounds she did not pull her weight.

Henry noticed the low battery icon warning and plugged in his laptop. He put a small black and white stuffed zebra, Zedith (Edith's stand in), onto the blue screen. He checked the chroma key to make sure the blue screen looked correct around her fur. Fur was tough to key around with his current software and lighting setup.

"Okay, Edith, we are ready for you."

Edith responded telepathically, "That felt more like ten minutes."

Henry crossed his arms and dropped his head.

Edith caved and sauntered over to the blue screen.

"Fine, what do you want me to do in the scene?"

Henry softened, "Well, what I want to do is to have a conversation with you in front of our viewers and show them how we communicate. You know that would be life changing, right?"

Edith knew exactly that. She liked their lives, did not want them to change, and had told him countless times that it would invite trouble because the world was not yet ready. Henry was annoyed but remained driven. "Let's focus on the scene at hand."

"At paw, you mean?"

"Yes, fine. The scene at paw."

He tapped his laptop and showed her the Klaus Nomi edit they were working on for "You Don't Own Me," which was, in their shared opinion, hilarious for a cat to cover. Edith admired Klaus's artistry, and Henry was happy to do something unexpected. Edith told him to add a lipstick filter to her face to sell the post more. Henry was surprised; he leaned towards being a consistent purist. Edith was savvy when she spoke to him and knew how to manipulate Henry into doing what she wanted.

"Yes, okay you probably know best."

The ease in her voice set the trap—Henry's self-confidence unraveled. He said he could try a couple of things, just to see. He also wanted her lip sync to be closer to perfect, but she was the movie star. Edith had a real handle on the uncanny and knew when to be more cat-like. She had command over the English language in all of their telepathy and never explained how she seemed to learn it so quickly. Edith suspected that if Henry knew more about the situation and had a fuller grasp on the mechanics of their communication, he would exploit the knowledge for financial gain. She was not wrong.

Cats are excellent judges of character, and ones as adept at telepathy as Edith had an even higher emotional intelligence. The fact that cats were largely assholes had nothing to do with a lack of comprehension. Henry liked to think he wanted his world to change, but like cats, he did not deal well with change. Therefore, Edith had her paws full with Henry and performed too much unpaid emotional labor. She knew he would be a world-famous pet psychic given his innate abilities, in conjunction with the evolutionary leap in consciousness he had undergone. But it would be his undoing. She did not think the world was ready to embrace someone like Henry. She studied Jackson Galaxy with him. White, Cis, Straight, Married, Recovered Addict, and Rock Star. Henry was none of those things. Henry was an absolute treasure, but he was way too ahead of the times. And timing mattered.

Edith always had the upper paw when he grew impatient. She cut off telepathy, cold shouldered him and acted coy, like she was a regular normie cat incapable of anything more. She was stubborn, lazy, and would take things out on furniture if pushed too far. Edith was also beautiful and knew it. She traded on her looks and Henry always came around to doing things her way.

8

Julia wore headphones and played music as she exited the plant-free zone at Franklin's house. She was unable to shake her interaction with the hedge but managed to finally explore the neighborhood. There were a number of old Craftsman houses, but otherwise it was an architectural mishmash. A woman walked a large beagle across the street. Julia was unsure if she should nod or smile. She decided to make eye-contact, but the brown dog pulled the woman in the opposite direction. Julia observed a couple watching television in one house and a man lifting weights next door. It was quiet. The kind of quiet that costs a good bit of money and requires yard maintenance.

Why were hedges so judgy about houseplants? They seemed to be equally under the green thumb of the man. Julia resisted looking too closely at vegetation of any kind but it was difficult. What the hell was she supposed to do with yards at every turn? She noticed a phenomenon in the near distance, a greenery-free concrete roundabout, the kind of oasis she needed in her life. Unfortunately, someone had beat her to it. There was a man seated on a bucket next to a second bucket. An aspiring drummer? No drumsticks. Julia used her headphones as a prop to avoid interaction and turned off the music to see if the roundabout was free of plant chatter. Success.

Julia noticed a torn-out foundation of a former statue. She wondered if it was recent. It seemed to be. She looked it up on her phone. Local news images showed teenagers toppling a statue of enslaver Junípero Serra. Benches and flowerbeds were destroyed too. Headlines revealed a neighborhood divided over what to do with the area. She would have to remember to ask Franklin if he was around when that happened. She tucked her phone away.

Avery leaned forward on the bucket. He tried to get her attention subtly at first and then with an exaggerated wave. Julia acted more annoyed than she felt and lowered her headphones. She asked him what he wanted. He was curious about the shattered foundation and wanted to know what she learned.

"Do you really needed me to tell you?"

He was embarrassed and apologized, said he would look it up later. Empty whip-it canisters rolled by like tumbleweeds. Julia decided to be generous and told Avery the former statue was just another man who did not need to be remembered. She sized up the area and noted its carceral feel. She asked Avery what he was in for.

"You'll judge me," he said.

"I'm judging you already." She raised an eyebrow.

Avery was reluctant. He had been seated for hours, and she was the first one to ask him what he was doing there. She took a seat on the bucket next to him, leaned in and said, "Do tell."

Avery told her about the orb sighting, how the roundabout was the location where he moved his arms and the UFOs followed his direction. He felt like it was an important location. Avery was concerned what the neighbors would think of him being there all the time. It became clear that both of them were new to the neighborhood.

Avery tried to guess Julia's age and wondered if she was too young for him. Julia picked up his vibes and removed her jacket to show more skin. She enjoyed being looked at, and the roundabout was well-lit. Avery suggested that the orbs would return any moment. Every time he said "orbs" she pictured perfectly round tits flying overhead.

He startled her when he leaned over to say, "I am glad to finally have a witness."

Julia tensed, "I should not be out here tempting fate like this. I have enough on my plate already."

Avery offered to walk Julia home. Julia countered that she was willing to walk *him* home, but Avery failed to jump on it. Julia stood and put on her jacket. She was bored and thought he was weird. Avery got up right as she pulled headphones over her ears. He was more attractive standing. Julia thought it was because of his height or posture. In either case, he seemed slightly better looking and was clearly interested in her. However, he did not know what to say. Julia was younger and he was unsure if she would consider him sexually. *His* interest seemed like a given. How could it not be?

Julia crossed the street and Avery followed.

He called after her, "Sorry for my delayed response. I am embarrassed about where I am staying."

Julia laughed, "My most recent home was a van, and before that, a small room behind stacked merch boxes off a communal hallway with fourteen housemates."

Avery softened, "I am forty and just moved into a guest room in my mother's house. Her girlfriend lives there too."

The hedge behind Avery laughed like it was the funniest thing it had ever heard. Julia found the hedge rude. She offered him a deal, "I will show you my orbs under the condition that you not talk to me on the way to your house."

It was strange but doable. Avery consented to her terms and walked slowly with his hand outstretched behind him to lead the way. Julia played music on her headphones and ignored his hand. He tried to play if off, stretched his fingers, and shoved his hand in his pocket. Julia found that she enjoyed humiliating him in slight ways. She would like to do it again. Avery glanced at the roundabout as they circled towards his mother's house. He worried that he would miss the next UFO sighting but felt compelled to go with Julia.

Avery hoped she would remove her headphones when they arrived at the house. Julia did not. She noticed bushes and hanging plants along the front porch. Social mores were not her concern. Talking plants were. Avery took her by the hand and pulled her into his room. He let go, but remained in the doorway to make sure they were alone. The house was quiet. He felt like a naughty teenager. He relaxed and shut the door behind him with a click. Julia perched at the foot of the open couch-bed. She was young and beautiful. Avery's palms began to sweat. He told himself to be cool. He had a hard time looking at her. He felt shy and kept some distance despite his attraction. He leaned against the desk. Julia removed her headphones.

"You can speak to me now."

"About what?"

She shrugged. "Are we perverting your childhood bedroom?" Avery clarified that it was his mother's place, and her girlfriend Catherine moved in a year earlier. His mother was a professor and a photographer. Avery stayed away from the arts but followed her into academia. Julia picked up on a vibe and asked if he liked Catherine. Avery was torn. "She's a badass curator, gallery owner, art-world type." He massaged the back of his neck. "She seems to think that I need to toughen up."

Julia's eyebrow arched. "Do you?"

"Who doesn't?"

Julia leaned back and shook her head, "Oh, I don't know, I prefer soft and pliable."

She removed her jacket and laid it down in a seductive manner. She enjoyed the heat of his attention, but it was all rather stupid. Why had Reggie forsaken their nuanced penumbra for a simplistic man who was just another Ikea lamp? Dime a dozen, she thought.

Avery offered her something to drink, then specified, "Wine or beer?"

"Are you trying to get me drunk?" Julia unbuttoned her shirt. "I'm almost parched." She paused in a liminal space with her cleavage showing. Avery wiped his sweaty palms on his pants. Julia held steamy eye contact and built the tension. Avery stared unmoving like she was a deer that might run. It was hard to believe his luck. Any moment it would surely backfire. Julia had control over a mediocre white man, and it was intoxicating. She had never gone with the flow like this before. His nonthreatening demeanor, and fear at what she might do to him next, was not lost on her.

Julia stood, reached for his hand, and placed it inside her bra. She placed her other hand on his belt buckle and unlatched it. Avery leaned down to kiss her, but she stopped him.

"Too intimate."

He was confused. "And this isn't?"

She shook her head. "Uh-uh, this is fun."

She slid the leather belt out from his pants, turned him around and bent him over the desk. She slipped off his shoes and pants. His boxer briefs were concealed by his shirt like he wore a dress. She felt playful and hit his butt with the belt. Avery turned his head to look back at her. Julia shoved his head back towards the wall and pulled his hair. She pressed against him and ran her knuckles on the outside of his briefs along his ass crack. His breathing grew shallow. She felt entertained. She looped the belt around his neck and choked him for a moment. She softened the grip on the belt, buckled it like a collar then guided him to the door. She slapped his ass. "You're cute. Go get us some drinks now." Avery felt electric.

A watershed of dopamine cascaded into Avery's bloodstream as he padded to the kitchen. He was lost in speculative notions and wondered what was it like to be a hot girl in high school or college and also have Julia's confidence. He would have been a dirty slut in the best way. He was sure of it. Would he have gotten pregnant? If so, he would have had an abortion. Did he want to have Julia's abortion? Was that a disgusting thought? Probably. His next thought was that men were terrible and gross. He was a stupid man and had disgusting thoughts all the time. His youth was perhaps wasted. He was trained to show and cultivate a profound respect for all women and girls. He tried his best to become attracted to other boys, all to please his mother. He was well read, and knew it was so much more interesting to carve out a life far from the confines of heteronormativity. Now, sadly, here he was, middle-aged, cis, not gay or even bisexual, to everyone's disappointment (self included), and still respectful of women. Something that had once been a cringeworthy notion was no longer one, it was a must: a midlife crisis classic. He was officially ready to be counted in. He wanted to be objectified by Julia, but he was not even a worthy object, merely a vessel full of privilege ladled onto him like honey, pooled over his body from the gods on a daily basis. All that sweet access, respect, authority, power, to be overrated and fail upwards. He loved it, would never give it up or trade it for the world. But it would be fun for Julia to tie him up and take whatever she wanted. She should punch him in the face. He bet she would slap his face during sex if he asked nicely. He actually *was* soft and compliant and horrified by the racing thoughts that ran compulsively through his ego. More importantly, was BDSM epigenetic? Was kink transferable by bloodline? Was he his mother's son and why had all this submissive longing lain dormant until tonight? Did it have anything to do with the UFOs? Did he want his anus probed?

In the dimly lit kitchen, he pondered what may have been unlocked during his intimate contact with the orbs. He opened the cabinet and lowered two wine glasses onto the slate counter. He snapped to reality when he heard, and then saw, Catherine crying at the kitchen table in the near dark. Evil made noises in the back yard. Avery's hands flew to his neck. He undid the belt and tucked it into his palm. He pivoted to bolt away when Evil appeared with a broom and a broken piece of terra cotta. They locked eyes.

Evil, feeling caught herself, launched in. Catherine had an episode. Catherine rolled her eyes at the word "episode." What, was she suddenly the lead in a television series? Evil suggested that Catherine's herbal cigarettes were laced with something, PCP perhaps? Avery was confused and asked if people still used PCP. Catherine lit up. "That's what I said!"

Finally, there was common ground between the two. PCP was dated. They could be a family and build from there. Where did Evil get PCP? Avery's wheels spun. Evil asked Catherine if she thought it was a psychotic break or mania. Was there any personal or family history? Catherine was unprepared to have a substantive conversation in front of Avery. Avery was incredibly unhelpful. He exclaimed that they had watched the film *Tarnation* by Jonathan Caouette, which featured a laced joint, and perhaps that where she was getting the PCP idea. Evil, a yes/and kind of person, found that, yes, it was possible and also not useful.

Catherine looked at Avery and asked if he had a rando in the house, someone from an app? Avery played stupid. He wanted to will her question away. It was not personal. He did not mean to be a dick. Catherine pointed at the two wine glasses, evidence that he was full of shit and that he knew what she was asking. The vague exchange angered Evil. She demanded that he answer Catherine's simple question. Avery nodded his head and said, "Umm hmm," like an eight-year-old girl hiding a stolen, half-eaten candy bar. Catherine was embarrassed for him but also upset. He explained that he did not meet her on an app. Evil asked where he met her. Avery did not like being a diversion from Catherine's possible psychotic break. Broken pieces of terra cotta and soil were all over the kitchen floor. That seemed far more pressing than his sudden libido explosion. Avery said he met her in the neighborhood. He told them that he was surprised they were being so uptight. Besides there was soil, leaves, vines, and broken pots all over the kitchen floor. He tried to communicate that the woman in his bedroom was simply someone that he met in the neighborhood who offered to walk him home.

He really did it with that one. It sounded preposterous. Catherine looked at Evil, Evil turned to Avery and cocked her head, "I think we need some ground rules for everyone's comfort, mister."

Avery took it as a slight. "House rules? That's a first. What do you have in mind, mother?"

"Go collect your random and we'll get back to you on the rest."

Evil went into the yard to get some air but pretended to clean.

Julia was restless. Avery's folded suitcase was on the floor by a small closet. His clothes spilled out like a well-traveled sandwich. Books tumbled forth from the tote on the desk, but Julia lacked any curiosity towards whatever he carted around. More curious was how uncurious she was feeling about him. The fun died an unremarkable death. She sat up and pulled herself together. She failed to outrun her emotional life by thrill seeking. Right then, as if sensing her erotic laments from afar, an audio message pinged from her phone. It was Reggie.

"Yes, I feel like I am hallucinating ... Cuz you said you never wanted to hear from me again. So, do you want contact or no contact? I can't hold your boundaries for you!"

Julia wanted to evaporate or self-combust, whichever was faster. Another message slid forth. A thirst trap selfie of Reggie, wearing only a crop top and thong, in a full-length mirror. Julia was overwhelmed. She shoved the phone into her back pocket. She needed to move her body, get it relocated far from the lackluster guest room in Avery's mother's house.

Julia explored the hallway. She heard annoyed women in the near distance say something about ground rules. Julia was amused that Avery got busted for bringing her home and smirked. She turned towards the artwork on the opposite wall and got dizzy—she had seen this work before. Her eyes darted and she held her breath. A photo of a pierced tongue in a vice. Butch women giving each other stick and poke tattoos. A large family portrait of a heavily tattooed bull dagger in a leather vest breast-feeding. That same woman, a bit older with a teenage son, Avery. Evil Fated was Franklin's neighbor? Avery was her son? Julia whipped out her phone and snapped pictures like she was Stasi. She could not get caught, let alone run into mommy or mommy's girlfriend! Or did she *want* to get caught at large in MILF city? Ugh, Avery was a total boner killer conflict. She had to ghost him and reset this whole paradigm. She ran into his room (Evil Fucking Fated's guest room btw) and grabbed her things. Her heart raced. Julia glanced over her shoulder as she slipped out of the front door like a gleeful spy.

Julia ran at full speed and dashed across the street. She was just in time to hear some hedges perfect a choral round to a Cat Stevens song. Julia was confused by the conventional music tastes of greenery. She asked the night blooming jasmine on the next gate.

"What's with the soft rock?"

"It started as a joke, but now it's seasonal."

She nodded to be polite and pulled on her headphones. The wisteria overhead and chimed in, "We miss birdsongs. Not enough birds."

Julia typed Franklin's address into her phone and learned that it was only a three minute walk. A stone's throw. Julia booked it back to internet stalk Evil Fated. Avery mentioned academia. Where did she teach?

Avery returned to his bedroom sans refreshments. He tried to come up with the coolest way to explain that it would be better to do this another time. He would make sure to say that he had a really good time and wanted to see her again. He was spit-balling language, but it became a non-issue once he saw that Julia was long gone. Of course she was a flight risk. Why did he offer her a stupid drink? He never even saw her orbs! He decided to run outside and check the sidewalk just in case. She was already the next block over and had her headphones on. He called her name and suppressed his urge to wave his arms wildly to get her attention. Avery took a few steps in her direction, but within those first footfalls, six orbs flew overhead. It was a subtle flyover, but they tapped into his psyche, like a frequency shift on a static radio dial. He knew they were back. Julia was far away but he could still catch up to her. Then again, she had made the decision to leave without a word, and now he had more important business than tending to her whims. He chased the orbs, ran to follow their glowing light. He tailed them all the way back to the roundabout.

9

Evil Fated taught at the same school Julia would apply to within five days and three hour's time. Julia had never realized she could look at an art school's faculty and use it as an impetus to apply, but it made a tremendous amount of sense in hindsight. Her higher education had commenced. Franklin had suggested art school after Julia expressed an interest in photography. Julia's "expressed interest in photography" was on account of Reggie, who loved having her picture taken. Julia enjoyed taking pictures of Reggie so much it felt compulsive. At the time of Franklin's offer, Julia had wanted to end their phone call as fast as possible. He was such a new and intimidating presence in her life. So she ran with photography. She loved it, but did not understand it as something she could pursue as a career path by attending an esteemed art school. She did not even know you could go to school with that, well, *focus*. Everyone she had known in the arts seemed to do the most, multi-hyphenates, the whole lot of them.

Julia favored Polaroids in a controlling manner that made her seem like an artist. Unfortunately, despite her devotion, she still lacked the required number of portfolio items or an artistic narrative beyond an ex-lover and a former weed trimming job. She also had an ongoing auditory affliction involving but not limited to the musical stylings of plant life. Julia reviewed the application requirements. She was thrilled to learn that recommendation letters were no longer part of the selection criteria, and she could use her photographs for the work samples. If Polaroid was good enough for Warhol, it was good enough for Julia. She would have to hustle to make it all pop. If she focused on the portfolio requirements that night, there was a chance she could submit the entire application on time. Julia glanced at Evil Fated on the cover of the book on Franklin's coffee table. Front door, side door, or back door? Julia wondered how she would enter Evil's life. She ditched her phone in the living room and went to the bathroom to check on her bath.

Julia's foot turned bright red in the scalding water. She kept it there, added her opposite foot then lowered her body onto her bent knees. She was scared with good reason—she might burn her vagina off once it dipped beneath the steamy surface. Nobody wanted that. Julia hopped from the tub and ran ice cold water over one leg at a time until her skin color returned to normal. She let icy water fill the little space that remained. It was not enough so she hung out naked for a bit. Her first instinct was to take a selfie, but her phone was in the other room. She applauded her instinct, felt it affirmed her life's direction. She also knew she was coddling herself, but it had been a day. The shadowy bathroom was lit in pink and amber, an ambience she brought together with candles nabbed from many corners of the house. She promised herself to remember to blow the candles out after her bath regardless of how stoned she got. It would be tricky, but she would try. That was really all she could do anyway. She would die trying—conceptually speaking.

It was time to look her future in the face, and smoking weed made that face funny. There was no way she would become too serious before she turned twenty-eight. Franklin made her promise to try and enjoy the years leading up to her Saturn Return. He was an astro gay or queer in the way that astrology was a required language. Franklin advised Julia to live it up, because from his experience, certain things were less cute after thirty. She should get away with as much as she could before then. She had a hard time listening to anything familial or paternal or brotherly or wise. She liked the part about having a pass to have fun and was uncertain about any cut-off for whatever "certain things" he meant. She did not ask him, *Like, what?* His ageist hot take did not square with the deal he struck around her school application. Something not fun at all. He did not require her to gain admission, just to apply, ideally to the art school he suggested, but that part was up to her. She decided to wait for three days to ask for his help, because she could not bear his sudden enmeshment in her life. It was too foreign. His house-sit was more than generous and everything else felt extra, especially him. Franklin was extra. His cat book was weird. She would ask him to do a final edit on whatever she cooked up with little time to spare. It would deny him the chance to suggest vast sweeping changes without seeming like a jerk. Julia cracked the window. She had plenty of weed—no need to hot box herself.

She stepped into the warm clawfoot bathtub with a lit joint in her hand. Candles flickered across the floor. It was blissfully quiet. She had tired of listening to audio on her phone to drown out chatty greenery. She had not smoked weed since she arrived and yet, all the plants were still on their shit. It seemed unrelated. She might as well enjoy her mid-twenties. She closed her eyes and pictured Evil Fated's hallway. She wondered what it was like to have your own body of work on display. It was probably more exciting to have work up in a museum or bought by a collector or something. Having a home lined with art that you made or acquired, or was given to you by a friend seemed like the best part of being an artist to Julia. She sensed that knowing what you liked from a place of understanding art seemed like a really cool trick. Julia did not know much about that world, was still only learning what she liked, and remained full of intrigue. She wondered what it was like to own a home.

Franklin had done well for himself by his forties. He had weird kitschy art all around his house. Would she ever own a home? What was it like to live with a son and a sexy partner who was also a badass gallerist curator? Julia subtracted twenty-five from sixty-two (having gleaned Evil's age from the internet) but it felt too complicated stoned, so she rounded it to thirty. There was space between them, decades even, three ten-year-olds like paper dolls holding hands side by side; but also, time folded onto itself with Evil's photographs. Her work was timeless and of a time, which made it all even more captivating, and her captivating and ageless. The way she created work that reflected her life was inspiring. Instead of following that inspiration onward towards usefully generative ideas for her portfolio, Julia thought about the way gay men engaged in intergenerational sexual relationships all the time. Right at this moment, she could throw a rock from the bathtub and hit a twink on his knees licking some silver fox's leather boots. Evil should be the recipient of a good shine too, and she was after all, only a stone's throw from Julia's bath. Julia was not much of a bootlicker but it was not out of the question. She plunged beneath the water with her joint held high above sea level.

Julia's phone flashed with an urgent astrology app notification. Chiron sextile Venus. Wounded healer drops by for some sugar.

Julia dried her hand off to skim the fuller report about her sudden luck, a chance to overcome injury. Julia's internet dive revealed that Evil was a Leo. After any heartbreak, Julia cleansed her auric field by sleeping with someone totally different from the person she was getting over. Astrologically, physically, and above all else, aesthetically. Reggie was her age, femme, anti-career, feral, a Gemini, and currently dating a man with a van. Evil was older, ambitious, established, a parent, and unlike anyone Julia had ever met. Even if Julia had not yet met her—progeny notwithstanding—it felt clear that weaseling her way into a ménage à trois was well above her pay grade. The limp joint clung to her lower lip as Julia squeezed soap to bring bubbles into her life. She wondered if she could be a normal person, not all hot and lathered over Evil. After her internet lurk-a-thon, and in consideration of Catherine, Julia's best move was to hone a chaste good student vibe. She had a snowball's chance in hell compared to someone so sophisticated who also likely trafficked in some aspirational next-level bitchiness. Even so, it was exciting to see that Evil was with an all-business femme who had some serious style. Meow. No, nothing romantic would happen. Julia just needed a little sexual frenzy as fuel to apply to school and honor her deal with Franklin. Free rent in exchange for applying to school. She took another hit. She could reign in her limerence. Historically, she was neither a creeper nor a home-wrecker.

However, if she was going to be a good person about all this, she was entitled to one Evil fantasy in the bath. That seemed fair. She would then release her lusty intrigue for a more respectable future as a photographer seeking tutelage. The best revenge against Reggie would be ambition turned into something material like an art degree. Julia remembered the unexpected thirst trap text from Reggie. Her heart twisted itself up into a poorly tied knot. Julia imagined standing behind Reggie, reaching around her bare frame, fingers along her waist, smashing Reggie's stupid cell phone into the mirror, shattering it to pieces. Her mind zoomed over to Avery. What a mess! She counted back from seven to one to slip into her allotted fantasy.

Fade in: Julia appears alone, adrift in the Fated hallway after discovering that Evil was Avery's mother. In this version, she imagines herself fully naked. She finds the kitchen, enters with the gait of someone wondering why the wine is taking so long. Three sets of eyes fall on her naked body. She performs genuine confusion, Avery never mentioned that he was not home alone. Apologetic, she retreats. Evil and Catherine are not far behind. They stand in the doorway of the guest room. Julia pulls on her bra and underwear. Psychic sapphic tendrils form a consensus. Yes. Julia would go upstairs and be placed on the sling in their bedroom as punishment. She was bad, very bad, and had followed a strange man home. How lonely and thirsty she must have been to do such a stupid thing. She was stupid and bad. The bedroom walls were clad with pro dom accoutrements. All three of them were dressed in matching black leather aprons, nothing else. Julia deserved a good paddle, or should she paddle them? Julia laughed. Her fantasy was too ill-informed. She had no clue who was a top or a bottom or what their dynamic was, and matching leather outfits had gone too far. She continued to laugh. Her stomach unclenched for the first time since the rest stop and the sinking feeling she had almost gotten used to was finally gone.

Julia was high after her bath, but mellow about it. She was inclined to believe that her state of mind was perfect to take a chance on being outdoors without her headphones. She was on drugs and therefore plant chatter was almost pedestrian. Julia did not want to bother with the hedges and their presumptuous nature.

She was on the market for something more akin to wisdom or guidance. The oak tree in the backyard seemed trustworthy.

She approached the oak tree, humbled by its size. It was very attractive and had a Venusian quality, a kind of beautiful otherworldliness. She asked the tree how it was doing and let the oak know that she hated the book *The Giving Tree*. Julia made it clear from the outset that she was not asking for a boat or a mother. She had no plans to rob the tree of its life force or ask for anything beyond a conversation. She insisted that she would be grateful and thankful for the tree. She wanted a mutually beneficial relationship with the tree and in fact, if there was something she could do for the tree, to let her know. Julia grew a little emotional because *The Giving Tree* was probably the first time she had encountered a concrete depiction of why the earth was doomed. It was likely a more innocent read in the '60s, but by the early aughts she was growing up in a world of stumps left behind in the wake of thankless men with too many boats. She was also emotional because of her own reckless behavior. She admitted that she had a bad reputation and was regarded by part of the yard of as a plant-killer. Julia felt terrible, remiss about the carnage. She was self-conscious and apologetic. It was really embarrassing and hard to admit, but she wanted so badly to be able to trust the tree's outlook. She did not want to hang all that on the tree—too much emotional labor, and she was not the oak's problem. Julia sat down and leaned against the large trunk. In her mind she kept saying *sorry*. She did not even remember what she wanted to ask the oak or how she planned to frame her questions. She felt sorry for the way the world treated trees and for her own crimes against greenery. She chose to be irresponsible instead of arriving at the house-sit on time. She would have had an extra month to apply to art school, not just a few days.

Julia wept at the base of an oak tree in Franklin's backyard on a weeknight. She did not remember what day of the week it was, but for some reason she knew it was not the weekend. The oak seemed to suggest that she was overwhelmed because of her lack of portfolio items and had mapped that distress onto a probably unrelated, evolutionary leap in consciousness. Julia perked up at the psychedelic discourse. The hedges were more lowbrow. The oak was deep. Julia asked if the oak was for real, or if the tree was just messing with her because she was high. The oak was older, considerably exhausted by the ongoing drought, and not one to mess around. Julia was unsure about her recent leap in consciousness and wanted to know if she was losing her mind. The oak had not anticipated that Julia would go right in and expose the hidden fear she was trying to evade using old playlists. Julia shared that she found nature super compelling but lacked any real relationship to it. She was not much for hiking and camping. It did not make sense that she was suddenly able to chat with an oak tree. It was far easier to imagine that she had lost her sanity.

Moved by her candor, the oak took pity on Julia. The tree had not accounted for the way her physical contact would feel. Julia caressed the tree a little absentmindedly at first. She held onto its roots like hands and sought comfort. The oak had reached a point in its life in regard to humanity where acceptance felt more worthwhile than judgement. It was something the oak had gleaned from Franklin's response to his father's sudden death. Franklin was on a call with a friend right after he got the news and said something like, "I just got to the point where I had to accept my childhood for what it was, same for my dad, because anything else was a lead balloon." There was something about the weight of the sentiment that encouraged the oak to lighten up. That said, though the oak was not ready for anything even close to friendship, Julia's tendency towards avoidance seemed to trigger something inside the oak, an anxious feeling, profound upset at Franklin for barely spending time in the yard before leaving without a word. Franklin had love-bombed the oak and then, when he got depressed, remained indoors, nary a hello. Julia could feel the oak's confusion. She stroked the oak's puckered bark and said Franklin was a bit self-absorbed. She owned that she was too, but they had shared a narcissist parent who was really terrible to Franklin. His own abandonment issues had also put him on the anxious-avoidant spectrum.

The oak conveyed that she understood this intellectually, but that did not make it feel any better. Franklin had gone to therapy, dealt with reparenting work, and even started dating a few people in a healthier manner before he left the country. But he never seemed to take the tree's experience into account. He appreciated the oak's beauty and had a puffed chest about sharing his yard with his dates. The oak was a bit underwhelmed by Franklin's choices in that realm. He took the oak for granted, an oak growing ever weaker and thirstier because of the drought. It seemed a bit basic to lack compassion about the climate, to be so self-involved. The oak believed landscaping had marred people's ability to value the health of plant life as something more than a style choice. Plants and trees that were not doing well "looked bad." It was all aesthetics. And don't even get the tree started on what birds are going through right now.

Julia told the oak that Franklin sounded like a real jerk. She also shared that she had avoidant tendencies too and did not want to disappoint the oak. There *was* something smothering and needy about the oak's energy. Julia wanted to say something about that but didn't want to be rude. The oak stopped her right there. That was all Julia's projection. The oak did not have any skin in the game with

Julia. She was a bit of a hot mess from what the oak could tell. Someone totally unwilling to risk vulnerability in her work and, while she might get accepted to art school, she probably would not make full use of the opportunity.

Julia did not like being called out by the oak but was impressed. She wasn't one for therapy, but if someone read her to filth, she could work with that. The smothering vibe was gone, and the pair coalesced into a chill reciprocity. Julia relaxed into the oak's perspective. She saw the backyard and felt the vibrant exchanges occurring all around them. Everything was so alive! It struck her that she had just processed with a tree. It may have been the most radically honest relationship she had ever formed. Definitely one of the best dates she had ever had. The oak was reluctant to go any deeper at present. It was all rather new, and it was not like they were doing hard drugs together. Life takes time and time was different as a tree. Julia felt far more trusting of the oak than the hedges or houseplants. She also wondered if there was more than one truth regarding the emergence of her recent abilities. Julia wanted to know if the oak had any ideas for her portfolio, but the oak had tired from all the mental energy. Julia yawned. She leaned back and shut her eyes.

The oak shifted Julia's perspective on what attending art school meant. She should get something out of it and to do so meant putting herself on the line. Her portfolio should be a rigorously honest account. She had to include Polaroids from the weed farm and her former throuple. She needed to shoot the dead houseplant grave and the oak tree. She would frame the recent work with a memoir quality and thread plant life throughout. Evil Fated's work spoke to her because it was so personal. Sharing her application with Franklin for his feedback would be a major issue because she did not want him to know about his dead plants. She could avoid sending him the full portfolio, or forgo his help entirely. She only needed to prove that she submitted her application.

* * *

The following day, Julia branched out from the oak, a bit overconfident. She approached an *aloe* plant and pronounced aloe like a hello, as in, *a'lo there*, but then second-guessed herself. She coughed and hunched her shoulders, quickly followed up with a low-key, "Hey, what's up?" as if the plant had missed her cartoonish approach. Honestly, the aloe plant did not know Julia from Adam. There was a prickly vibe between them. Julia was uncertain if it had anything to do with her houseplant killing history. Just because she had one new tree friend did not make her Julia of the fucking jungle. She had to build relationships with a few more flora for her project, and unfortunately there was not much time. She seemed self-serving because she was, and it was showing. Telepathy sucked. Julia was embarrassed. The plants had her number. She stammered, "Cool, cool …" and then ran onto the porch.

She closed her eyes and tried to relax. She had to be in a kind of neutral and perhaps even genuine space to get what she wanted. There was no way around it. She would have to be forthcoming and just go for it. The plants were wise to her. It was maddening. Julia preferred running rings around people and being a quick study. She failed with plants on both counts. She noticed a splotch of dirt on her boots. She spat on her finger and wiped it clean. It was a relief to enact such a pure action without an ulterior motive. Julia was grateful for all the rocks around the porch. There was a mote of calm before the rest of the yard gave her, the plant murderer, what felt like dirty looks. The front yard was not as judgement free and flexible as the oak tree.

A particular hedge was not in the mood for idle chit chat when Julia approached it with her camera. She felt like something was off. Julia said, "Hello hedge, how are you today?"

The hedge was like, "How am I? How am I? Do you not hear that lunatic with the leaf blower? What is with humans and leaves? Do you hear that?"

Julia acknowledged the loud sound but did not know how to comfort the hedge. It was not the kind of foliage she could gather into a warm embrace. She tried to distract the hedge and also move things along. She leaned over and whispered, "Listen, remember when you said you would tell me why I can suddenly communicate with plant life? I'm ready to hear it."

The hedge did not have the faintest idea what Julia was going on about. The hedge was not good with faces or people for that matter. The hedge lived in the moment and swayed with the wind. The leaf blower crescendoed in a way that seemed like a direct threat. Julia felt awful hearing the hedge put it that way. She thought about the leaf blower's relationship to power. She took up her camera and framed the hedge in the foreground, the orange leaf blower looming in the background. The resulting composition reminded her of a certain televised presidential debate. The photo was evocative. It depicted an inequitable power dynamic. It was almost as if Julia wasn't faking being a photographer for her portfolio, but actually creating work.

10

Three orbs dropped beneath a cloud in perfect sync like a magic trick. Avery held his phone to the sky to share a live feed. There was a lot of cloud cover, but the orbs found a way to remain visible. Avery tracked them with his phone like a wildlife photographer filming a rare condor. In no time, UFO and UAP enthusiasts and curious onlookers from around the world tuned in. The number of viewers crept towards the millions. Avery had never been part of a global phenomenon before. His body felt at least ten degrees warmer. He wondered if it was anything like how athletes or musicians felt like in a packed stadium, being seen by so many eyes yet unable to see the audience in return. He felt like he might piss himself, but then the orbs disappeared behind the clouds for a lengthy time. He prayed it was only momentary, though it looked more like the orbs were gone. Avery flipped the camera to himself, in order to maintain his viewership and take ownership of the encounter. He wanted to be affiliated with the orbs and thought it would be more believable with his presence.

"How about those geometric feats?" He sounded goofy and second-guessed taking a sports commentator type approach. He would not do that again. He shared with his viewership that it was his second encounter in the same location. Always the feminist educator, Avery asked his audience if anyone out there had also had a similar experience. Did orbs return to the same places on a regular basis? What did they think? The audience was mostly quiet, but then *UFOwen5* typed a comment to say they had heard about repeated encounters, but they were rare.

Avery decided it would be really exciting if they could work together as a collective to try and will the orbs to return. He asked if there was a certain shape they all wanted to focus on to call the orbs back. Maybe there would be an encore, they could certainly try. He decided on a triangle, but he let the hype build. He lied and claimed that the triangle seemed like the most popular shape in the comments.

"Let's all focus together on calling them back and imagine them appearing in a triangle."

Avery returned the camera to the empty sky. He was uncertain if anyone would watch a blank feed more than a minute, if that. He also was unclear if anyone else mattered in this scenario, or if he, alone, could summon the orbs.

He concentrated and felt a potent mix of fear and longing. If this daring game and its high stakes paid off, his world would be forever changed. It had already changed of course, but he needed it to change in a way that was more about *him*. It was true that he was just a man making a live feed from a broken roundabout in his mother's neighborhood, but he swore he had a real relationship to the orbs. He felt bonded to them, as scary as it was to admit. His body hairs were back at attention, but the skies remained quiet. Avery was too excited to look at his phone. He had no idea how many people out there were concentrating on the triangle shape. Each quiet moment that passed made him weary that the orbs were taking too long to return to the roundabout. He could sense them but had no idea how much longer it would take. Right at his tipping point, as his self-doubt got a leg up on faith, he turned the camera back to himself to end the feed, but the orbs reappeared. He recorded as they formed double triangles in the sky. Three crafts made the larger shape first and then a smaller triangle inside it with three more orbs. Avery audibly gasped. Given audience participation alongside visible proof, Avery's feed was far superior to anything he had seen online, and he had never felt so accomplished. The UAPs disappeared.

Avery looked into his phone's camera as a tear rolled down his cheek. Hearts flooded his feed. He sat down on a plastic bucket. "Wow, I really need a moment, but follow and message me." Everyone was kind. Some asked if they could bring him camping gear so he could stay at the roundabout. Others offered to join him. There were comments in so many different languages that Avery was awestruck by the global experience he had created along with his new orb friends. It was a new beginning and the start of a significant turn in his life.

The roundabout remained quiet for the next hour. Avery was scared to look at his social media account. He became worried about orb enthusiasts flocking to the area. He would need to get the neighborhood gossip from his mother. Avery had already mentioned the statue being removed and all she said was good riddance. Avery suspected she helped tear it down whether directly or indirectly. He would have to press her until she talked.

Avery wondered if Evil was still angry with him for bringing a girl home. Evil would worry if he stayed out all night after the way he left things. He needed to go to the house. Tomorrow he would research local UFO groups and seek out legitimate academics that worked in the field. He did not want to be a joke. He felt serious about his relationship to the orbs. The timing of his life and the events that led him to be exactly where he needed to be felt unshakably dire. It was only a feeling, but it grew stronger and filled him with purpose.

11

Henry set up his blue screen with more ease than usual and decided to shoot behind-the-scenes footage. When he clipped his phone into the tripod, he had what felt like an epiphany, he had never done a live feed. He thought it might be interesting to record the setup for a few minutes before the shoot. Henry always edited behind-the-scenes footage before posting it to have full creative control. It was the real reason he never recorded a live feed, not because of a failure of imagination or that he needed some great epiphany. In fact, his "epiphany" was really just a subconscious drive to create his desired chaos.

One of the lights cast an irritating shadow and Henry worked tirelessly to fix it. He repositioned two lamps and forgot that he was recording. Early viewers thought the live feed was an accident or that it had not started yet. Henry darted across the frame wordlessly. Hardcore Edith fans stuck around because she was in frame, only much farther away than anyone wanted. Comments about her distance from the lens piled up without Henry's engagement. Henry needed Edith to move a little bit to the right. Henry asked politely at first, but Edith was her usual stubborn self. Henry told her to move her ass, and Edith responded that he should shake his own money maker. Their usual banter escalated into campy vitriol, little insults laced with sass that amused them both to no end. After a heated back-and-forth, Henry cackled then threw his head back. He saw his phone on the tripod and his face fell like melted wax.

Henry shuddered. It must have seemed as if he had spoken coarsely to his cat, like a terrible stage mother. He shame spiraled and made a split-second decision that would haunt him. With a need for absolution, and without considering the bigger picture, Henry raced over to his phone and told his rapidly expanding audience that he was telepathic. He had a true connection with Edith and really, she was sassing him back. He confided that yes, he was coming out as a cat psychic. It only worked with Edith, though he never really tried to communicate with any other animals. After a joke about monogamy, he tried to explain that the pauses between his quips were filled with her acerbic wit. She never wanted him to tell anyone about their relationship because she didn't think the world was ready. It was only at that moment, when he shared her feelings on the matter, that they registered as important. He looked sheepishly at Edith.

Her boundary had been clear, and he knew that boundary well enough to restate it en masse. Henry had to push things forward because it was his livelihood, both of theirs, the ad revenue and few sponsors were their meal ticket. Henry asked Edith to please come over to the camera and sit on his lap so that they could show the world their true selves. He wanted her to show the world how unique their collaborative efforts truly were. He wanted Edith to have the credit she deserved. Edith's glowing green eyes narrowed. It was some serious next level bullshit. Henry told his audience that Edith was worried about what would happen if he went public.

Edith stood, stretched, maintained eye-contact to raise Henry's hopes, and then walked off camera. She then turned back to let him know, *Well, now you've really done it.*

Henry tried to address his ballooning live feed. Thumbs downs, boos, commenters telling him what a disappointment he was. He ended the live feed with an emotional meltdown apology, then doubled down on being a cat psychic, that Edith did not want anyone to know. That was why she was withholding her talents, not because they lacked telepathy! He ended the feed and clicked off his phone. It was over in a matter of minutes. Henry sought comfort from Edith. He apologized. He got on his knees and apologized again. She watched him from behind a pair of dress shoes underneath the bed. Henry begged her to come out so they could process. She wanted no part of it.

Edith was notoriously stubborn. She cut off communication with Henry. She spent her time sleeping or fake sleeping. She had warned him that the world was not ready. She offered clear directions for his own wellbeing and was ignored. Edith understood the implications around the particular timing of his choice to go public. This was not the right moment, neither his ambition nor his will made a difference in the grand scheme of conservative climates. He should have done what she had suggested, been an artist or a cat behaviorist, a trainer even. His decision to come out at this moment unleashed a different ball of yarn entirely. And that ball rolled farther and faster than either of them could imagine.

Henry was in a tailspin. He thought live feed videos disappeared once they ended. Unfortunately, one of his viewers had recorded his live video on their own device. That former fan reposted it with every hashtag that Henry had ever used, plus some that described the video with words like *meltdown, crazy, abusive.* Henry lost thousands of followers within the week. He tried to get the app to delete the recording. The app claimed to be in the process of reviewing his request and said someone would get back to him soon. He knew that meant the video had viral engagement, so there was limited incentive for them to do their job. He had a sense that it would all blow over in a few weeks after something else went viral. But the reason it was not dying down was the most embarrassing hashtag ever, a play on the Dog Whisperer—#catyeller.

* * *

When Edith went missing Henry thought she was still in the apartment. He had really fallen apart after the viral video. He wore the same black romper and red slides as each day blurred into the next. He went to the bodega to get ice cream every so often. On those trips he felt like a disgraced starlet. He wore oversized sunglasses and a hat wherever he went, mostly just out to get some air in the near-by park. He was unsure what he would do for a job now that his dreams were dashed. His regular and reliable ad income from his cat videos increased dramatically at first from the rubberneckers at the crash site (his only solace), but then it fell off to a random pittance. Henry was going to have to get at least one regular job. It was crushing to go back to the life he worked so hard on social media to avoid. Edith could have saved the situation, but she chose to let him fall. He was hurt and needed to process. Regardless of being an indoor cat, Edith was never around anymore. It was like living with a phantom creature that ate and pooped. She was intentionally quiet in the litter box. She hid whenever he was around and withheld all affection. Henry was doomed to feed and clean without reward. He was in cat purgatory. He started to research Bergman films for their next project, but it made his heart ache. He was uncertain when or if they would ever collaborate again.

When her food remained untouched until well after dinner, Henry got worried and thought she was unwell. He figured she was still intent on hiding from him and gave it a little more time. Edith did not eat breakfast. She did not eat dinner. Around two in the morning Henry was frantic. He searched his apartment inch by inch. He decided to make missing posters once it was clear that she was not in their home. He tried to figure out how she could have escaped. There was the cracked kitchen window with a ledge that continued around to a fire escape. There was the bathroom window that would have required Edith to jump into a tree. That seemed like too much effort. The only other possibility was that Henry was so out of it that he could have left the door open after returning from a late-night ice cream run. If she lurked in the shadows when he entered, she may have darted out without being noticed.

* * *

Henry knocked on doors with his posters. He hung them around the neighborhood. There were some reports of coyotes, but he found that a little hard to believe. Edith was a woman about town. She was probably in someone's care, making a point about how well-liked she was. He had to hold onto that image rather than one of her being hit by a car or something worse. Henry was too scared to tell the online community about his situation. He did not have the strength to hear mean things or how he deserved this. He had already been stung by #freeedith. He could not handle anyone celebrating her disappearance.

12

Evil had had too much coffee and no idea what happened in the last three portfolio reviews. It was hard to remain present in a dark room with a single wall projection. The faculty had gone over prospective student materials for hours on end and she felt like a bad person for spacing out so hard. The good news was that the standouts always stood out and they already had a very talented pool. It was Evil's turn to lead the room through the next group, applicants who had all listed photography as their primary medium. She told everyone to take a ten-minute stretch break outside before diving in.

Instead of taking in the beautiful day and having an actual break, the workaholic, overworked artist faculty jumped into their devices to check emails and grab dopamine from social media. Only the smokers seemed to be a liberated class, aside from the whole tobacco addiction thing. Evil looked at her phone, too. No texts from Catherine or Avery. She tried to think of something to say to either of them, but it was the middle of the work day. She hoped Avery was making good use of his time. Catherine burned the candle at both ends. It was best to leave her be unless there was an emergency because anything else led to confusion these days, especially with how much she traveled for work. Evil felt a little lonely and jealous of the artists Catherine was focused on. She needed to find her fire again. Evil did not want to go back to the portfolio review. No one did. Break time offered a false notion of some kind. One that she had to disabuse. Evil blasted "9 to 5" from her phone and did a little jig towards the building.

Julia's digital photo with flowers in place of pubic hair invited a bit of intrigue. The next image was entitled *The Last Throuple* which got a laugh. But more than any other one, the hedge with an orange leaf blower in the background sparked actual dialogue. In the end the room was divided about Julia. A few agreed that her voice was inconsistent. Evil made a case for a narrative with themes around power and play. No one wanted to read more essays than they had to. It was late in the day and the applicant pool was bloated. The faculty members who had their own rogue hopefuls sided with Evil, and Julia advanced to another round. Evil clicked to the next artist. It was a photo that featured handwritten text carved into vomit. Evil was excited about the batch of applicants and exclaimed "The kids are alright."

* * *

The next morning Evil had to read more essays than she cared to count. Avery was nowhere to be seen and Catherine was in Berlin. Evil filled the French press with enough coffee for all the three of them; regardless, she needed it. Her solitude was peaceful and easy to savor. She ate yogurt and a few fistfuls of granola. Grocery shopping could wait. She opened her laptop and entered the applicant portal. She kept a pad and pen handy because that was how she preferred to think.

Evil started with photography focused students because she felt the most connected to them. Julia's personal essay opened with her half-sibling, who had been kicked out of the house for being queer when she was too little to understand, but she held onto his belongings as secret subcultural treasures that eventually shaped her worldview. She jumped to her parents' recent funeral where the two reconnected as adults, his encouragement to pursue photography, then a weed farm, a break-up, and a big finish citing Evil's work as her reason for applying to the program. Julia's art practice essay covered similar ground but focused on risk-taking and memoir-style photography with an interest in plant-telepathy and portraiture. Evil felt tender about Julia. She found the plant stuff a little odd, but the rest of the application was captivating. Evil never went to art school herself. She wanted to fight for Julia, a self-taught weirdo who was in competition for a spot with artists from elite institutions or had at minimum been serious about their work for many years. It would depend on the cohort. Evil felt drawn to Julia and not only because of the flattery.

The coffee was long gone. Evil clicked to another student in the portal when Catherine's unexpected video call became a welcomed reprieve. Catherine was hot from drinks with Hito Steyerl. They met to discuss a show that Catherine was in the initial stages of curating. Their meeting had gone well, and Catherine was heading back to her hotel early. Evil thought she looked stunning and wished she were in Berlin so that they could go to her favorite dungeon together. Evil tried to say as much, but Catherine was in work mode, so she did not register the flirtation. Catherine had back-to-back meetings as her new grind. She would be out of touch given her travel itinerary. Evil told her not to worry because she was swamped with portfolio reviews for new admissions. Catherine asked about it to be polite. Evil told Catherine about Julia and how she was unsure if she had a shot this time around. Evil mentioned how her own work had been the inspiration for the young artist to apply to the program. Evil brought up the portfolio reviews because she was jealous that Catherine crossed the globe to meet with Hito. Evil wanted to sound like a real draw too.

Catherine suggested that, if Julia did not get chosen for the program, Evil could hire her as a studio assistant, or to perhaps hire her either way. Evil needed an assistant and had been putting it off. It might as well be someone she found compelling and who was a fan. Unspoken was the fact that *not* hiring an assistant was one of several ways that Evil had recently gotten in the way of her own career. Catherine's art world ascension made Evil feel like she had taken a wrong turn. When Catherine traveled for work, that tension grew even more palpable. Evil shared her hope that Julia would be admitted into the program. She went on to share about the portfolio piece with handwritten text carved into found bodily fluids. It was political and not without humor. As Catherine crossed the lobby, she said she would probably lose Evil in the elevator. And then she did. They texted a smattering of emojis as placeholders.

13

Franklin has had trouble concentrating ever since he saw the now infamous video of Henry's meltdown. He grew obsessed with the unexpected direction Henry's real life has taken and wondered if it impacted his novel. He wrote Patti as the more intuitive character, the character far more likely to be psychic and have telepathic ties to her cat Vegas. Psychic ability was not in his storyline, and it did not strike him as something thematically relevant to masculinity and cats. If being psychic implied sensitivity then maybe he should include it? Franklin would need to do a serious overhaul if he wanted to thread it into the narrative. How important was the unexpected life turn of real Henry to fictional Henry? It was a question that made Franklin lose all focus. His word count goals went unmet, and Club Mate made him anxious. He was frustrated. It was a fictitious novel that drew inspiration from a total stranger with a social media account and a cat. Franklin was the one who created the rule about Henry's posts and could just as easily stop using real Henry as a prompt. It was fiction! Why was that so hard to accept?

It was unclear if Franklin needed to stay tethered to real Henry rather than his own imaginary Henry. Before real Henry's meltdown,

Franklin had been busy crafting a climactic scene and was more than halfway into his current draft. The story was built on a situation where a bunch of copycats imitated Henry and Patti's art project and made it viral. The characters learned about the copycats, and the viral nature of their work, when they boarded a train. Henry wore an Edith mask over his face, and Patti was in her Vegas mask. They intended to do a photo shoot for their collaborative project riffing on David Wojnarowicz's *Arthur Rimbaud in New York* series. Henry and Patti came cat face-to-cat face with a sea of people in cat masks in the subway car. It was shocking! Patti and Henry were polarized in their responses. Patti hissed then dominated all the cat masked people. She was spontaneously recognized as the cat people leader. The people in cat masks tailed her and moved like a feline gang from car to car. Patti/Vegas hissed and meowed and scratched at anyone in her way. Everyone on the train joined in the moment like a mass hallucination, except for Henry and a few people faced people sans masks who did not get the memo. Seated on a bench alone, Henry removed his Edith mask and was just a person again. He got off at the next stop and caught a train back home.

The section was a major part of the narrative and character arcs. Franklin was curious how he would rewrite the story if either primary character were a cat psychic. He could introduce latent psychic abilities after the climax, but that felt slipshod. It also made him more worried about real life Henry. He had no relationship to Henry beyond social media likes. The insurmountable issue was that real life Henry and fictional Henry had both become very real, and so had both Ediths.

Franklin checked his socials for any trace of Henry since the #catyeller incident. There was nothing. He decided to send him a DM and create a new rule. If Henry ignored the message, he would continue his book as is and disregard the psychic thread. Franklin would release real life Henry and Edith in a literary seance. But if Henry did write back, he would have to throw some psychic abilities into the narrative mix to see what shook out. Franklin planned to keep his message brief.

* * *

Henry's face was illuminated inside a dome made from blankets. He scrolled through his emails and texts to make sure he had not missed anything regarding Edith. There were a few tuxedo cat sightings that Henry responded to but none of them were Edith. Two were black cats. It was devastating. Henry scanned his DMs to check if anyone had seen Edith despite the fact that he continued to keep her disappearance offline. He read Franklin's message which was unexpected to say the least.

On a whim, Henry confided to Franklin that Edith was missing and that he was too scared about the internet fallout to ask for help. Franklin responded that he was around if Henry wanted to talk. Henry was surprised that he did want to talk and called Franklin. He liked that Franklin was a writer with a solid following and hoped that he would have sound advice. Henry was swinging on the final bit of twine on his last rope. Franklin caught him. They talked for over an hour. Franklin shared a bit about his novel and how Henry and Edith inspired some characters in the book. He made it sound both flattering and light.

Overwhelmed, Henry worried about Edith and was still unsure whether or not to reveal online that she was gone. Franklin surprised himself as well as Henry when he inquired about the cat psychic stuff. He wanted to know if Henry had exchanges with other cats or if his gift only worked with Edith. Henry admitted that he had never engaged with other cats. Although the bodega cat might have chatted him up once or twice. It was hard to say. Henry was unsure if that was useful. He feared that Franklin was going to encourage him to adopt another cat, but Franklin only wanted Henry to ask the cats in the neighborhood if they had seen Edith. Henry warmed to the idea but said he was scared because he did not know if it would work. He wanted to know if he could keep Franklin in the loop either way. Franklin agreed and hoped for Edith's return.

* * *

Henry almost wore a trench coat to play detective, but his heart was not ready for fashion. Instead he wore jeans and a t-shirt, which was very out of character. Talking with Franklin had helped him form a game plan before he left his apartment. On his way out, he noticed Edith's missing poster was missing from where he had taped it to the wall next to his door, just like her. Henry was uncertain how to engage with the local felines. As soon as he was outside, it was apparent that his first stop should be a Ragdoll cat in a window on the first floor. The curtain was shut behind the cat, so there was a barrier in case someone thought he was a burglar or a pervert. He was definitely a pervert, but that was beside the point.

Henry tried to still his mind. He planned to ask the cat in the same casual way he had grown accustomed to talk to Edith, then realized that his communication with her ran much deeper. He had to recall how their first telepathic exchanges began. Unable to stifle an urge to document his first attempt, he took a picture of the blue-eyed fluffball. Henry calmly tucked his phone into his neon belt bag (his broken heart was still able to accessorize for function) and contemplated what he wanted to ask the Ragdoll cat, but only in his mind. He brought Edith into his mind and tried to project her image and personality to the cat through a specific memory. The cat licked its paws. Henry was ready to go back home, having failed, but then he received a response. It came through a combination of images and feelings that amounted to "Haven't seen her. Ask the indoor-outdoor cats, maybe try Little from next door, she knows everybody, but don't trust the ferals." Henry thanked the cat and asked where to find Little. The blue-eyed cat looked over Henry's shoulder across the road. Henry followed the cat's gaze. He saw a small brown and white tabby playing with a plastic cap. Henry knew better than to rush across the street to confront the cat. Instead, he had to act like he did not notice Little then cross in a random way as if he had somewhere else to be. Henry circled with plausible deniability between them. He spoke to Little from afar using only telepathy. He tried to mix up the way he expressed himself with the style he got from the Ragdoll cat. Pretty much, he said, "Excuse me, are you Little from the building across the street? The cat in that window thought you might be able to help me. I'm looking for my girl." He projected out a slideshow of images of Edith that pained his heart. He missed her so much. Little had not seen Edith but said she would keep an eye out. Henry thanked her and took her picture.

Weather-worn missing posters made him feel gutted. Where the hell was his baby angel? He messaged Franklin and sent him the pictures of the two cats who had not proved to be worthwhile leads. Franklin was surprised that Henry was so nonchalant about being a cat psychic. It seemed like a big deal to find out his abilities went beyond Edith. Franklin asked what it was like, if the cats had different voices or personalities, what the interactions had been like, were they similar to Edith or different? Henry had not given it much thought. He was too upset about Edith to step back from what had happened. He realized that he did not trust his "psychic" interactions with the cats. It could all be a made-up story in his mind. There was no way to fact check his interactions without actual details. Not until Edith was found could any of it be considered "real." He was in a nightmare scenario with only himself to blame.

A thick grey tabby cat slunk along the side of Henry's building. It was a fast-moving ball of fur, twice the size of the one in the window, and looked like plush tumbleweed. There was something shady about the cat. Henry grew suspicious. The cat knew something. In the movie of his mind he yelled "Follow that cat!" Henry hugged the building then darted towards the alley. Henry wondered if Edith was an alley cat now. It was hard to fathom. It did not seem like her scene. Dumpsters? Loud bottles careening down the street or weird smelly puddles in potholes? Car engines and trash collection? Not his Edith. It seemed impossible yet here they were, Henry tracking leads and Edith on the run. A runaway. *His* runaway. He was a terrible parent. A wicked stage mother or a tyrannical conservatorship overlord. #freeedith #catyeller He had exploited her, crossed her clear boundary and now what? Henry did not see the large grey cat anywhere. He looked behind the dumpster and up the fire escape. He thought he saw a tail disappear into an open window, but it was hard to say. He called out, "Edith, here kitty kitty! Come home baby! I'm sorry!" Henry swore he felt her presence. Her judgement. She knew he was looking for her. Or maybe that was all in his mind as well.

* * *

When Franklin read Henry's text that mentioned sensing that Edith was nearby, it sparked an idea. Franklin thought like a writer and considered where fictional Edith would have gone. Fictional Edith would not have gone far; unless someone took her somewhere else, she was still close to home. He asked if Henry had put flyers under all of his neighbors' doors? Franklin understood Edith as intelligent and a bit snobby. There was no way a cat like that was going to hang around the alley for scraps. If Franklin were Edith, he would have stayed nearby. She probably did a dry run to case the building at least once, possibly more than once, and left when she found a mark. Someone that could be conned into taking her in but easy to escape from if it was not the right fit. The other question was abduction, if Edith had misjudged and wound up with someone that would not let her go or she could not sneak out. If Henry thought Edith was close, she probably was close, and if Edith was in danger, Henry would surely sense it. Franklin also thought it might be a good idea to make the flyers smell like Henry and Edith, to entice her to return home.

Henry listened to Franklin's advice because it felt good to have someone else tell him what to do. He rolled a stack of flyers around her cat bed and cuddled with them in his bed. Henry slid scented flyers underneath all the doors in his building. He went to a nearby botanica and bought a dressed candle to protect Edith, to call her home.

It was sunny out when Henry called Franklin in the late afternoon, Franklin was already in bed. He decided it was their time difference that made talking to real Henry feel dislodged from reality. Henry shared his recent accomplishment. Henry- and Edith-scented flyers had been placed under the doors of all twenty-nine units in his large four-story building. And he had a seven-day candle burning as a backup measure. Franklin was encouraging, but also in a mood. He was creatively constipated because of his real investment in what should have been fictional characters. It was hard to work on his book while the real Edith was at large and he was uncertain about how to approach the cat psychic storyline in his novel. He needed a sign.

"Did you speak to the cat in the window again? Or meet any new ones?" Franklin heard his voice sound pushier than he meant it to, but underneath that push was heartfelt sincerity.

"I learned something today. The building next door does not allow pets. Unless someone is breaking that rule, she is definitely not over there and that limits the search area." Henry was no longer sure why he called Franklin. It was not much of an update. He realized he had called simply for the attention that Franklin provided. He was wary that Franklin was mining him for his novel. It was mutually transactional, but for some reason Henry felt annoyed. Franklin's long-distance attention was a poor substitute compared to the light that filled his world in Edith's presence.

"How is the cat psychic stuff going? Do you feel like you are getting better at it?"

"Is this for your book?"

"I don't know yet. I feel curious about all of this. I wish I knew what it was like to be able to communicate with cats the way you can. Sorry, we don't need to talk about it." Franklin fell silent. He was full of regret. His romantic interest in Henry derailed because it was inappropriate to flirt while Edith was still at large. Franklin, the chivalrous hero, rode in on his fictional horse to be a vessel of encouragement. He did not know what to do with his attraction. It took a strange turn after he admitted to Henry that the fictional characters in his work were homages. Where do you go from there? Uncomfortable City, by the looks of it. Franklin never found any way to pivot towards romantic intrigue. Henry was an emotionally distressed starlet who fell from grace. Culture chewed him up in real time. In the silence that next befell them, Franklin sensed not only had his romantic aspirations collapsed, but any semblance of friendship had flatlined. Franklin hoped someone would intervene with paddles in hand and yell "Clear!"

Henry adjusted his left earbud after scratching an itch. "Listen Franklin, whatever story you have in your head about my life is probably far more interesting than reality. Honestly, I don't care about being a cat psychic. I was woefully misguided. Wrong, even. I wish it never happened. All I want is for Edith to come home! She is what matters. Who cares about social media? I haven't posted a thing and here I am, just fine without it—aside from missing her. I just want my baby back. I don't care about anything else. It is good we inspired you for your book. Write your stories, write whatever you want about us. Fill up the multiverse with Edith, she deserves more worlds than I could ever give her. I could not even keep her in mine."

Tears streamed from Henry's eyes. He clasped a pillow to his chest.

A persistent meow at the door made Henry yank out his earbuds and drop the phone onto his bed. Franklin heard the cat and Henry's running steps. The apartment door creaked. Henry cried, "Edith!"

Franklin thanked the universe. He paced. He was ready to share his great relief when he heard rustling. Henry raised the phone and ended the call without so much as a word. Franklin stared at his phone for several minutes. His face reflected in the black mirror looked distraught. He self-soothed. He told himself it was all for the book, just part of his process and he could finally continue without worrying about Real Edith or Real Henry. Franklin channeled the fresh emotional rawness into his work. He wrote about Andy Warhol, loneliness, and twenty-five cats named Sam.

* * *

Edith slept in a warm sunny spot by the window. It was impossible to know where she went in her dreams. Most hours of the day she slipped away into parallel realms. She lived a whole other life with her eyes shut. Henry failed to ask about her dreams and regretted it. He was grateful for her reappearance and did not initiate contact using psychic channels. He dialed their lives down instead. He became an average cat parent. He did the same for his own life. His month away from social media had cleared his head and cooled his ambitions. He stopped picking up his phone to scroll absent-mindedly after the first two weeks. It did not take too long to regularly forget where he had left his phone. His apartment no longer doubled as an art studio, and Edith remained free of any demands on her time. Henry worked and enjoyed the few hours of downtime after his barista shift and before bar-backing at night. It was a little like playing house. Both of them too shell-shocked from their separation to depart from routine domesticity.

Henry stopped bringing men home. He found that it was easy enough to enjoy himself at the bar. There, he was a multitasker and used his break time to enjoy trade in a stairwell by the alley. An archway afforded privacy with a nook large enough for multiple bodies (stuffed beyond capacity on one lusty occasion). It was his secret garden without the garden. He hosed it down when he cleaned the rubber mats. "Good enough" was his new worldview. It was fair to say that Henry had shut down the most sensitive parts of himself to avoid any poetic need to create content. He siphoned his drive to produce art into his sex life. If anything, he was now a choreographer. There was his nighttime dance and early morning routine. When he saw cats on Main he veered in the opposite direction.

* * *

Franklin stopped using social media. The residency was temporary, and Franklin needed to commit. There was his current outline and an urge to destroy it, as well as an unfortunate reckoning with time, that it moved only in one perfectly-paced direction. Tick-tock. Real life Henry and real life Edith were ink stains from a broken pen faded slowly off his skin. Franklin needed to seed a multiverse for Edith to roam and finish his manuscript. He typed at a furious clip. Where in the multiverse do cats go when they sleep for hours on end? Dreams or permutations of reality, windows open onto meadows, cats chase prey in grand cardboard-lined colosseums, mice and lizard marathons with surprise ambushes! And for the nocturnal beasts, secret forests to offer bird sacrifices in witchy rituals. Non-narrative. Experimental. Cats languidly explore other dimensions that are counter-productive and anti-work.

* * *

Henry handed an espresso and an Americano to a young couple who were still dressed from the night before. The pair seemed equally confused when a group of teens in cat masks pooled inside. Drip coffees all around except for the Mocha Latte Tabby.

"It's a little early for a stick up," Henry teased.

Mocha Latte Tabby paid for the beverages. The teens left as fast as they entered. There were more cat masked teenagers outside with placards. Henry tried to read the signs but could not see the scrawl from his vantage.

The young couple watched on. One of them, still a bit tipsy, guessed "Oh, they are like, protesting that cat psychic stuff, right? That's cool. I knew it wasn't just a social media thing."

Their date shifted uncomfortably, "Wait, wait, no, they are pro-cat psychics."

"That's what I said."

"No, you said protesting it."

"Don't cat 'splain me, man. It isn't even 7:00 a.m."

"Protest 'splain."

"You're lucky you are hot because you are annoying af."

The couple exited out the glass door. One of them glanced at Henry then, given the talk of cat psychics, did a double take after recognizing him.

"*The Edith and Henry Show!*" They pulled it up on social media to confirm before asking, as if Henry was a cardboard cut-out or a lowly barista, anything other than an actual human being.

"*The Henry and Edith Show*," Henry corrected as he made himself an espresso—it was going to be a day.

Roving packs with placards raced past the coffee shop.

"It's all coming down. You were like the Molotov, baby!"

"I'm an old. I haven't been online. I need you to translate whatever you are saying to me."

"You came out as a cat psychic. Everyone hated you and thought you abused your cat. Then all these teens started defending you and were like, "Hey, cat psychics are a thing." People were showing off their skills on social media, doing readings and stuff. Probably some cat psychic wannabes and scammers but definitely ones that were for real. It was big, like witches in 2019, like everywhere, you know? A cottage industry started with the pushback to clear your name—Henry and Edith are legit!"

Henry leaned onto the counter. He was rapt. "For real or are you messing with me? I won't be mad because this is the most entertained I have been in my whole entire life."

"No! Everyone was looking for YOU online. Check your view counts and your comments. People got obsessed. It moved on from finding you, to people coming out and saying they are able to talk with their cats, all kinds of people, all over the world, and like, so many teens that it was being called a cat psychic contagion. People were pissed you got run off the internet for being honest. That part really inspired the youth to be more open and claim it and offer readings. Then a few conservative parents caught wind and the satanic panic exploded. It's not clear why it is so threatening, but it became a thing. Now they are trying to ban cat psychic readings, cosplay gatherings, and any kind of monetary exchange. Conservatives are trying to outlaw the mention of cat telepaths anywhere near people under eighteen or something. They want to classify cat psychics as adult entertainment. They think telepathy is evil and the work of the devil. And you know, cats and witches and leftists, they want to shut it down, they don't want cats to have a take on what is happening in the world or any kind of influence. There are rumors of shadow bans and hashtag suppression. Also, cats are super opinionated. They had already taken over the internet but giving them a voice and real platform? Cats are totally encouraging the fight."

Henry was suspect, "That barely makes any sense."

"Yeah. I mean I am not a cat psychic but that is what has been happening on social media and in the streets."

"You want more espresso or another Americano?"

They nodded. The cafe shifted into a conspiratorial vibe, all of them caffeinated and high on gossip.

A few teens wearing t-shirts featuring cat laser eyes and "Pawer to the People" rolled in.

"Hey, can I ask you what is going on out there? My new friends told me a story and I only half-believe them. I have major trust issues."

"He's Henry dude. Like, *the* HENRY from *The Edith and Henry Show!*"

14

Avery arrived at the private university and felt sad about his life choices. He longed for the ivory tower to claim him, but as an adjunct, he was always a stepchild or a bridesmaid. Avery circled three lots before locating one with actual guest parking. He felt overwhelmed and rushed. He took pictures of his space, the lot, and the cross streets, in order to be able to find his car after the meeting. Campus sprawl plucked his time cushion bare. The swirling sidewalks were confusing and hard to navigate. He felt like an imposter but at least he had GPS on his phone. He was too anxious to stop and ask for directions. The professors had all agreed to meet Avery and found twenty free minutes to be able to say they met the "roundabout guy." Avery lost fifteen of those minutes being late.

He was sweaty by the time he recognized the three professors waiting for him under a large yellow umbrella next to the café, as promised. The near empty cups before them hosted remains of melted ice cubes in taupe liquid. Despite his own thirst, Avery introduced himself and jumped in. The professors complimented his live feed again and peppered him with questions. His sudden notoriety was the leverage he had used to get the meeting. They were old hats, not the jolliest bunch. Avery immediately regretted not making individual calls. He was misguided in thinking that meeting in person would clarify if these future colleagues were somewhere in his destiny.

Avery was disappointed by a shared lament about the state of UAP and UFO study within academia. Apparently, given a recent release of information from state agencies and declassified covert operations, there was a shred of renewed hope for funding and interest. Astronomy, philosophy, physics ... most science departments had zero plans to expand their fields to include ETs. As tenured professors with some overlap into paranormal arenas there was a bit of leeway, but all three agreed it was still fringe. There was a slow-going cultural shift. Legitimate reporting in papers of record had improved research opportunities. Support and funding were limited outside of government channels and private bankrollers. Those two channels meant less freedom of authorship in writing, research, and publishing. It was a heavily guarded space. There were gatekeepers, always. It was a closed system constructed to package facts and real documentation alongside disinformation, in order to keep things perpetually murky. Senator Harry Reid was their last congressional hope for transparent research. With his passing, it felt like change would have to come from outer space. Hollywood or the military sounded like the only potential meal tickets in the field.

Avery left the brief conversation deflated. He had organized the meeting to solicit encouragement for his unspoken plan to rejoin academia by pursuing a PhD in the field. He wanted the scoop on the best program and path, but found it a mostly uncharted, somewhat laughable, pursuit. Maybe by the time he finished his second PhD, the cultural climate around that discourse would be different, but more likely it would remain a joke until ETs landed in a very public way. And really, *that is* who he wanted to study under, not human scholars. Avery knew his days as a Women's Studies adjunct professor were over. He needed to move out from his mother's house as soon as possible.

* * *

As Avery drove home, his mind raced towards next climbs. He was a fan of autonomous zones. A large number of people had reached out to him by direct message, people who witnessed his orb interactions and were interested in meeting up. Would his mother kill him for starting an autonomous orb zone at her neighborhood roundabout? Was that his next move? It was not that he wanted to monetize his orb connection, but rather he wanted to expand it. He needed a way to re-center his world away from his mother's influence, but the orbs found him in her neighborhood. They were both part of this situation, despite his displeasure in another overlap. Avery felt ill. He decided to head back to the roundabout to have a think.

Avery parked at the house. He ran inside, grabbed a bag of snacks and a notebook. He changed his shoes and took off. As he approached the roundabout, he saw four colorful lawn chairs. His heart raced as he imagined Julia there with her friends. He considered what to do if it was a situation where his presence was unwelcome. He had never anticipated that someone else would be at the round-about. He should never have left. He had not given much thought to Julia since the orbs had engulfed his reality. When the people in the chairs became more visible, he failed to recognize any of them. As far as he could tell, there was one woman and two men, all around his age. The woman had long hair, one man was very hand-some, and the other one less so with a bushy beard. Avery wondered where the fourth person was and spotted a large van parked nearby.

He cleared his throat because he did not want to scare them. The trio looked at him and all smiled knowingly. The bushy bearded man said, "You must be Avery." Avery nodded and thought if he were more like Julia, he would have said, "Who the fuck are you?" but instead said, "Yep." They had seen his orb live feed and traveled to the roundabout. It was their van parked nearby and the fourth seat was for Avery. They offered him a drink from their cooler. Avery found all of them attractive and familiar. They were reminiscent of people from his past but like fifteen degrees off. It was a little strange. He could not tell if anyone was a couple or if they were all single.

The woman was called Sam, the handsome man was Xander and went by X, and the bushy bearded guy was Jay. They were in Joshua Tree when they saw his live feed and decided to pay the roundabout a visit. Avery asked if they had ever interacted with orbs before in such a direct manner and it turned out that they had. Sam showed Avery a video where she had set up LED lights in the desert in various shapes that the orbs mirrored back to her. The orbs did not look like much, not as clear or impressive as his live feed video. Avery felt attracted to Sam. It was unclear if she was dating Jay. X was definitely not dating Sam. Avery could tell by the way that he was cold towards her and also, X was way too stylish and attractive to be straight. The group shared a genuine interest in communicating with orbs. They swapped favorite videos that documented meaningful contact. Avery wanted to know what the shapes meant. He asked them if there were any more complex shapes or patterns, and about the maximum numbers of orbs witnessed in a contact.

There was a ton of mystery, and that was what drove the trio. They threw all of Avery's questions back to him as if he might know more than them. Avery found that silly. He was new here. Avery asked if they had ever attended conventions, what those were like? Every question that had ever occurred to him poured forth from his mouth. He was a bit self-conscious about putting strangers on a pedestal as if they were the ones "in the know," but they did seem to have been at it for much longer. Avery felt a kinship with Sam, in addition to his attraction to her, because she had a direct line to the orbs as well. The other men did not. The questions they asked Avery were mostly to tease out how he had communicated with the orbs, the difference in his two interactions, intrigue around the exact times that he had his encounters. They wanted to know what it felt like, and if there was anything beyond what they had witnessed on the live feed. Avery was unsure if Sam had given him a look—like, *Don't tell them everything you know,* or if he imagined that she had. He was unsure where to place his trust, or if that even mattered. He was not ready to trust anyone. Avery thought about the show the *X Files: Trust No One.* He tried to keep that in mind and left his answers vague.

Jay showed Avery their van. It was like a tiny house. There was one large bed, a miniature kitchen, and a compost toilet. Camping gear was stowed on the floor underneath the bed next to three tightly rolled sleeping bags. Jay made a pot of coffee using a solar kettle. The van was surprisingly clean, and it made Avery suspicious for some reason. It was too new and barely lived in. The instant camaraderie was also a flag, especially from Jay. In fact, Avery decided it was Jay that made him like feel something else was at play. He patted Avery on the shoulder and was the first one to make physical contact that was too familiar. Avery registered that he was wearing a wedding ring, something Avery would never have noticed without being touched. It felt calculated. Jay needed Avery to see that he had a wedding ring on, but Sam did not. Avery helped carry a stack of blankets and coffee back over to the roundabout. X outed himself as gay soon after.

Avery tried not to reveal how many inner alarm bells were ringing in his head. He was no stranger to cults—he watched documentaries, heard podcasts, and read books that explained how they operated. The main thing that always struck him was the way that cults attracted recruits by becoming a primary friend group to a vulnerable person. They would become your world, and you would have to join the cult or lose your world. Throw in a sexual relationship and it was even harder to say no to the circle of welcomed warmth. Avery probably seemed like a mark to the outside observer. What they did not know was that he was raised by a lesbian bull dagger who nurtured Avery to be a street savvy dyke who did not need anything from anyone else to get by in the world. He might be a sub, but he was nobody's sheep. He also did not require all his self-worth from his relationships. He learned not to do that by observing his mother, her many lovers and friends. He made a list of things he vowed never to be, and emotionally dependent was a hard no. Avery's problem was that he had inherited Evil's Achilles' heel and, sadly, his self-worth was tethered to his career. It was an American problem as well and a masculinity problem. His self-esteem was totally dependent on how he thought he was being seen by the world. Of course, no one was actually thinking about him much at all.

Sam created her own back-channel to Avery. He could not discern if she was manipulating him or if there really was a sparkle of chemistry. She asked Avery if it was okay if she set up some lights on the roundabout to try and communicate with the orbs after sunset. Avery was a fan of the idea and in no position to counter. X shared how he was hard at work on a sound wave frequency project in relation to the orbs and excused himself to continue his project in the van. X asked them to text him if there was a sighting. Avery was disappointed that Jay stuck around until Jay suggested that the three of them meditate together. He wanted to see if they could initiate contact through a group vision exercise that created a vibrational field. Jay seemed knowledgeable and focused. Avery appreciated the vibe shift away from him and towards the orbs. They all had something important in common, it was a shared goal, unbent towards any hierarchy. Sam, X, and Jay seemed autonomous and self-driven. Maybe it was not the kind of "group think" he feared. Jay had been interested in UFOs since he was a kid. He grew up on a ranch and there was some strange stuff that went on with the land as well as with cattle. Things that he did not like to talk about and will never be able to shake. Jay suggested they watch a little bit of Avery's video to harmonize with the orbs and then meditate on the shapes they had performed in the sky. He said to project a welcoming energy.

Avery relaxed into the group. They were grounded adults looking for connection. Jay was a bit awkward because he had not had the kind of contact that they had. He was trying too hard. Avery felt disarmed, or allowed himself to be disarmed, so that the meditation could work. He loved the idea that they had a van setup to track sightings and encounters. All of them were prepared to be there all night. Avery was self-conscious rewatching the live video feed of himself, but he focused on the shapes. He held them in his mind along with Sam and Jay. Avery stole a glance at each of them. They both meditated, eyes shut. Avery relaxed into the scene and envisioned the orb shapes, the double triangle. Sam played footsie with him.

* * *

It took three nights for the orbs to return. Avery had only been home to shower and change. The little pack that began with four lawn chairs increased nightly with curious neighbors. Onlookers circled the roundabout, unsure how to feel about the people lounging in its center. Avery suggested Sam arrange her lights into a double triangle, one smaller and one larger like he captured in his feed. Sam was able to set it up so that the lights turned on and off to mirror the symbol. He asked Jay if it was okay if they only meditated on this one symbol. He did not think the meditation or the lights were necessary, but tried to be community minded. With his quiet ambivalence, Avery sensed that he was subconsciously sabotaging the orbs' return. He overheard Sam say something about Joshua Tree to X. It felt like something had to happen soon or he would lose his new scene. The fact that they were all around his age, and looked uncannily similar to people he cared about, made it sting all the more.

Avery cleared his mind of bullshit. He was flanked by Sam and Jay along with six neighbors that meditated in a circle. Avery imagined triangles appearing, a small one on the inside, a larger one around it. He recalled the particular feeling from that moment. He was in awe and then devastated to be left behind. There was a flicker, a familiar sensation like a minor frequency shift. Avery opened his eyes and looked to the sky. Three orbs circled above the roundabout, mirroring its shape. Avery whispered, "You guys." The group opened their eyes and watched in awe. Avery said "Triangle" and made one with his hands like he was dancing the YMCA. The others followed suit, but Avery knew he was the point person. The orbs shot apart into a large equilateral triangle. Jay texted X. The door to the van sprang open and he raced to the roundabout.

Avery thanked the orbs using the fuzzy communication they somehow shared. They were trying to tell him something, but it was too public for Avery to receive the message. He felt like their communication might be intercepted and so, in a way, he had walled himself off. His paranoia was palpable. He wondered if the orbs were warning him not to be so open. He trusted that feeling, whether real or imagined. Avery decided to simply hold onto a sense of thankfulness. He was grateful and felt like he would burst if he did not express it. Avery wanted to know what was next for their relationship but knew the others were reason for caution. Once the orbs disbanded, everyone rushed to use the van's compost toilet. Avery ran home just in time to let his bowels respond to the encounter. Afterwards he crashed out hard in the backyard and did not remember a single dream.

* * *

Avery figured he had passed a test because of the way he was treated after the orb visit. It was like everyone's shoulders dropped a half inch, especially Jay and X. The neighbors that spontaneously joined the group returned to their lives with a story to tell at parties. The hardcore lawn chair quartet had a new dynamic. Avery remained unchanged in his feelings towards them, but everyone treated him differently. Sam continued to thread her mysterious needle, lingering gazes cut short like a thousand honey-dipped paper cuts. She allowed for occasional sparks that left Avery pining, regardless of his actual ambivalence. Avery found the group to be an odd gaggle. He was unconvinced that they were simply friends who shared a common interest. They felt more like work buddies or colleagues, a professional architecture undergirded a shallow friendship. His sense was confirmed when they told Avery they had a job offer for him, but that their supervisor was in Joshua Tree. A meeting was set, and Jay suggested they all head down there together in the van the next morning, Jay explaining that they would drive him back to the roundabout either way. Avery was cautious. He was curious. He had told them about his employment situation, so it was kind for them to try to get him work. But it felt strange to be driven all the way there and back. Avery asked, "Is it okay if I drive separately?"

His request landed in an unexpected way that disappointed the group. Avery wondered if they were willing to tell him more about the job, and said he would go in the van if he could get more information. Jay said that was not on the table. Avery offered to caravan or have any one of them as a car passenger on the way down. His concession returned air to a flattened atmosphere. The group was relieved. Sam jumped at the chance to go in the car, because Jay loved to drive the van and X had sound gear everywhere. More than anything else it seemed logical, but Avery remained hopeful that with some privacy, something would develop between them. They parted ways while Avery went home to pack.

Evil was in the kitchen revising a syllabus when Avery surprised her. He was unshaven and seemed more amped than usual. She was skeptical of his latest plans. He did not even know what the job was, only that there was a supervisor and UFO enthusiasts. It sounded made up, but he was excited for once. She pushed against her weird feelings and smiled instead. "Stay in touch, keep me posted and have fun." She wanted to be supportive. Evil was thrilled that he was taking a break from the roundabout. It was concerning, and while she didn't care what the neighbors thought, she also did. Avery had no way to reassure her that the trip would be fun. Avery was unsure if fun was in the cards.

His shower and a clean shave felt clarifying. Avery realized that he was anxious about leaving the roundabout for more than a night or two. He felt abandoned by the orbs every time they disappeared. He wondered what would happen if they thought he had abandoned them? Would they know he was in the desert or would their connection wane? No one could promise him it would not. Was any job in the world worth leaving the orbs behind? Avery did not think so. He needed to think. He did not even know what the job was but saw a group of people around his age gainfully employed and able to follow orbs. Why couldn't the supervisor do a phone call or video call with him? That was weird. His anxiety mounted. Sam texted to ask when he would be back. She was getting them road snacks. Avery's guilt won out and he felt like he had to go, especially since he made a thing about having his own car. It did give him some peace to know that, and it would be good to have Sam in a one-on-one situation.

* * *

The caravan to Joshua Tree was a little out of the ordinary. Never in his life had Avery driven somewhere with another car that was unwilling to be more than three car lengths away. He could not help ponder X's sound equipment and wonder if they were being surveilled. "Where did you grow up? Are you still close with any family?" he asked Sam.

"I don't like to talk about my past. I'm more … future focused," she deflected, then turned to face the horizon. Avery waited a few minutes.

"Do you like working with Jay and X? Is the job something you feel like you will stick to? Any clues as to what I am signing up for?" He asked in his most relaxed sounding voice.

"It's work," she offered, and then put on the radio.

Freda Payne's "Band of Gold" played and Sam sang along with the chorus. Avery thought about his ex then fantasized about Sam reaching over and placing her hand on his knee. Sam removed her sweater and her shirt lifted up. Avery could not resist eyeing her skin. His attention drifted to her hands and her mouth, her thighs, then back to her arm. Sam had a tiny stick-and-poke tattoo of rabbit ear antennas. Avery could not tell what it was.

"What is your tattoo? I never noticed it before?"

Sam shifted in the seat. "Why would you have?" She folded her arms.

Avery did not know how to answer. He pivoted "What was your first contact with the orbs and how did you come up with the LED call and response project?"

She relaxed with his new line of inquiry. Avery was drawn to the geometric shapes, and Sam was passionate about UFO lights and colors. He shared that together they were unstoppable and would be visiting the ships in no time. Sam whispered, "If only." Avery's heart twinged. He asked, "When they disappear into the sky do you ever feel left behind"? She nodded.

Avery pushed it. "I sometimes feel like there is a vibe between us and if I am mis-?" Sam's phone rang in her hand. She answered. The caravan needed to stop at the next exit to get gas and use the restroom. She ignored his question.

Avery was nearly done filling his tank when Jay approached him. Sam was still in the restroom.

"So, we need to do some work stuff on this next leg. It won't be too long. You're okay to fly solo." Jay turned before Avery had time to respond. He watched Sam cross the station towards the van. She looked defeated. Avery did not know if it was because he pushed things too much or if she already knew that Jay would request her presence.

Flying solo appealed to Avery's overactive imagination, which was growing more paranoid and suspicious as the caravan continued. He increased the distance between his car and the van and called his mother. He fell back behind a semi and used it as a shield. Evil answered. Avery was more honest this time. He turned on his shared locations so she could track his movements.

"Sounds like you need to decide if you are willing to work for a covert government agency or some billionaire with a penchant for alien hunting." She had a gift for tweezing his mental splinters.

"Right. Should I turn around and come home?" Evil was more curious than ever but tried to balance that with being a good parent. "If you feel in danger at any point, yes, but also, they already know where you live, they have your face and probably your DNA, so maybe just roll with it? At least it's not a band of raccoons. They would have emptied your bank account by now." She tried to sound more encouraging than she felt. She did not want him to be in danger but maybe it was all good life experience or would lead to a job or something. Avery felt like a fool. He had been so open with the lawn chair contingent. Higher Ed had its landmines, but nothing like this. "I do need a new career and maybe this is the path. Hopefully, I'm just being paranoid." Avery thanked his mom and hung up.

The caravan pulled off well outside of Joshua Tree; "JT" was merely a general area of reference. They drove far into the desert. It was extra dusty driving behind the van. His phone service ended, and along with that his shared locations. He followed them down a dirt road. Light orange dust clouds swirled in front of the windshield and rocks shot out from the van's tires. He wondered if his car would have a bunch of new dents as evidence or souvenirs or both. The landscape was vast. He could not see any homes or development beyond the well-worn dirt road. Occasionally there were smatterings of rusted wire on posts. To the trained eye they could be landmarks to find the place and probably were. They slowed to a stop near a boulder with a cow skull on it. Avery wondered if the buildings were underground or hidden in the rocks. X ran over and tapped on his driver's window. He handed him a tablet with an NDA on it. "Sorry for the late notice. We meant to do this at the gas station. You have to sign this, or we can't meet our Supervisor." Avery had an out but was too curious to draw a boundary now. He skimmed the blanket non-disclosure and nothing seemed under handed. He signed it. And off they went.

* * *

Avery was surprised when they arrived at a small grid comprised of twenty and forty foot shipping containers that blended in with the rocky terrain. He parked by a long light grey container with a conference room visible through the glass window that ran the length of its side. There was a large telescope on the same roof. The rest of the containers were more concealed. There could be countless employees inside and he would have no idea. There could be snipers with guns trained on him and he would have no idea. It was not long before Avery was seated inside the conference room with a view of his car. He was happy he drove and had had enough mental space to freak out without having to act calm until that moment. He was an easy mark, and this is where it led. He was nervous and excited. Sam, Jay, and X had disappeared.

The Supervisor talked like a character actor from a Cold War drama. She had dark red hair in a tight bun and wore men's Under Armour like she was training. She made reference to Avery's background and had questions about his connection with the orbs. Avery was told that he was special and his ability to commune and direct the orbs was rare. She called him an "Antenna." The fact that they made contact more than once made him even more unique. He asked if that upgraded him to a "Super Antenna." Avery's joke was too casual and fell flat. He tried to sound more serious, "Can you please tell me more about the antenna signifier?" The Supervisor was steely-eyed and declined, "No. We are getting off track."

It was a government outfit after all. The task force had ties that dated back to Roswell and worked under the US Military. They had expensive toys that he might get to play with down the road. The humorless Supervisor was surrounded by posters from *Alien Autopsy* as office decor. Avery found it tacky, given the official nature of the project, and the fake alien guts repulsed him. Jay, Sam, and X were agents in the secret task force. If he agreed to be the new hire, Avery would be on their team. Their prior interactions were all part of his vetting process, and they felt comfortable onboarding him.

If Avery agreed to be part of the unit, he would have to sign an agreement that limited what he was able to share with anyone. The Supervisor assured him it was standard practice. The additional NDA would be similar to what he had already signed, but more comprehensive. If he worked at Apple, he would have to sign something similar, it was just that the stakes were in regards to national security—like the fate of the world more than intellectual property. The Supervisor made him feel like he was being called to service. They also knew he was unemployed, living with his mother, and without any job prospects at the time. The Supervisor knew the academics Avery had met with after his orb encounter. These were small circles. She knew of his interest in a career shift. He could be employed to do what he was already doing, but he would have a chain of command. There would be orders that he would question but needed to follow. That was key and the real sticking point. He asked if he could sign the NDA to learn more, but still have time think about taking the job. The Supervisor responded, "I see what they mean. You ask disappointing questions." Avery felt tormented by that observation and would need therapy to unpack it. He felt swallowed up, like a capsule being digested inside the monstrous body of the man he had been raised to fight. It was THE MAN. The fucking STATE. Avery was torn about signing the next NDA. He was probably losing the rights to his own story, his individual connection to the orbs, and much, much more than that.

Avery's shoulders caved. "I don't know if I can do this."

"Do what?"

"I'm not sure yet but I think it might be best to not hear more or sign anything else."

"You want to leave? And then what?"

"If I need more time is that something that I can have? Are you going to be watching me?"

"We watch everything that interests us."

"And I interest you?"

"Less and less."

The Supervisor tapped her fingernail on the desk twice, stood up, and left the conference room.

Avery was unsure if he was free to go. His car was right outside. He did not see anyone around. Avery decided to act casual yet make a run for it.

* * *

It was unclear how much time had passed when Avery came to in his parked car outside of a tiny strip mall just off the Twentynine Palms Highway. It was dark out and the stores were all closed. He was confused. His throat was sore, and his nose felt like sandpaper. He tore a booger from his nostril, and the pain from little hairs stuck to the mucus was erotic. Avery rolled his head around. He was tight. He had a terrible headache, and the back of his neck was wildly sore. His heart raced. He found his wallet and phone. He did not know what happened. A significant wedge of time was carved from memory. His drive down was foggy. He remembered leaving the roundabout when Sam was his passenger. His headache pounded as he tried to recall anything at all.

A weird feeling washed over his body. On a hunch he grabbed his phone. He checked his photo album. All the photos from the roundabout with Jay, Sam, and X had been deleted. His recordings of the orbs were gone. His social media apps were deleted from his phone. He downloaded them again. He logged in, but his account had been deleted. Avery tried to look himself up on the internet, the orb videos he had made public, but his socials did not exist. He remembered the handle *AlienGuy666* and saw that the clone of his video was still up on that account. It was not a repost, but *AlienGuy666*'s own recording of the post. The UFO scene must have known this might happen. They were smart. Avery was not sure if any of this mattered in the grand scheme of things. Enough people had viewed the video; it existed, people knew.

He'd lost his ability to instantly be in touch with more than a hundred thousand international followers. He did not know how many followers he'd even had, because his time in the roundabout with Jay, Sam, and X had pulled him away from social media.

The agents had occupied his time, and he did not know when his socials and photos had been deleted. For all he knew that could have been before they left for the desert. In his notes app there was a phone number that he did not recognize. Avery did not want to call it, but decided to store it in his contacts. When he entered the number, it came up already stored as NDA. This freaked him out more than anything but also jogged his mind. He flashed to barbed wire and a dirt road. He signed a document on a tablet, did he read it? What did he sign? How was he so stupid? His head pounded. Avery coughed and started his car. He checked his text messages. Evil wanted an update asap. She was worried. Join the club.

He pulled off at a gas station. He bought burner phones, Ibuprofen, and a gallon of water. He texted Evil *don't worry*. In the movies, he was at the part where people throw their smartphone out the car window. Avery did not have that kind of disposable income. He rooted around the glove compartment and stole a paper clip from old receipts. He grabbed a pen from the armrest and wrote down the number and "NDA" on the back of the smog test envelope. He used the paper clip to remove the tiny SIM card but was unsure what to do with it. There was an X-acto blade in his armrest, so he stabbed the card until it seemed beyond repair. He threw half of the metal bits in the gas station garbage and kept the rest to trash elsewhere along his return trip.

* * *

Avery learned camping gear was stashed on the highest shelf in Evil's garage. She did not believe in organizing by bin color because it felt too constrained. Avery half-listened to her philosophical musings, but mostly just plundered at will. Evil watched him with a gnawing concern. His improvised plan to go off-grid seemed like something to push against. Instead, she made small talk about being socially conditioned to accept petroleum by-products. Her plastic bins were useful but not worth their environmental cost. She invested in black ones to conceal their presence—organizational strategies be damned.

Evil was scared, and he saw it in her eyes. He wished he could counter her instincts, be of comfort, but she was right to worry. He was worried.

"I'm reachable on the burner if it has service. I won't let it go more than a week without some kind of communication." He tried to sound like he had more of a plan than he did.

Evil did not like it one bit.

"Can we swap cars? I think that will help."

"Won't your disappearance raise flags? Being boring makes you unmemorable. Can't you just go back to eating my groceries, being depressed, and fake jogging? This feels too fast, unhinged."

"That's because it is. They probably put a tracker on my car. I need time to think. I can't do that here."

"So, you want them to track me?"

"Maybe. But so what? What are you doing that matters? They won't abduct you."

"Rude. Don't do anything too stupid."

She removed her office and studio keys from the keychain that was in her pocket.

Avery hugged her and placed his keys in her palm with a burner phone.

"Thank you. Love you."

He used his burner phone to call the one in her hand. She looked at him unsure if she was supposed to answer it, but he ended the call. "Now you can text or call if you get worried. If I take longer than a week to respond, you can worry then and only then. Remember that I am only on a camping trip. Or just pretend that I live in another city. We have not been in touch like this in years, but it will be like riding a bike. Out of sight, out of mind, all that. No biggie."

"I never thought that I would consider UFO orbs in the neighborhood as the good old days."

"Catherine will be happy to have her house back. I'm sure you will, too."

* * *

Avery loaded up Evil's car. He circled the roundabout one last time and attempted to telepathically exude a missive to the orbs. He would contact them from the woods. He did not know if his psychic message would leave the car, much less travel above the tree line to the skies, but he held it in his mind's eye. He was scared that they were in some kind of imminent danger if they didn't disperse. The chunk of time that was carved away from his memory made him feel violated. Avery was foggy on whatever happened in the desert, and he wondered what horrors Sam was involved in. She did not give him much to go on except a shared wish to hitch a ride with the orbs. It could have been a performance to gain his trust. He did not trust her anymore. He added a postscript to his message. He wanted the orbs to stay away from any LED outreach and the neighborhood roundabout. He pictured Sam's LED project and imagined a red blinking cross to warn them away from her.

* * *

Pyramid Lake was his first stop. He had been curious about the reservoir and Piru lake whenever life placed him on the Southbound I-5. It was a site of many drownings and seemed haunted; they even banned swimming there. He reserved a campsite off Hard Luck Road. As a literature fanboy he was not above the sway of a street name, and one so apropos was impossible to ignore. He arrived at the Los Alamos Campground with a good amount of time before sunset. An attractive blond couple in red swimwear and white sneakers played volleyball. It looked like a scene from a soft drink ad. Next, he passed a site where a family raised tents while kids played tag around an empty fire pit. It made him feel lonely and like he needed to have a dog to seem like an okay person. He was a white man in the serial killer age bracket. He wished aliens would come get him.

In the parking area, Avery botched folding up his paper map and was frustrated by its puffy resistance. It took everything not to crumple it into a ball. When he flattened the map to try again his eyes landed on Mount Shasta. He considered the spot a potential destination. He intended to stop for no more than a night or two in any one location but failed to book additional campsites in advance with a laptop or smartphone. Now he had neither one and spontaneity would likely prove punishing. He could probably head to Mount Shasta and figure something out. It drew the same UFO-friendly demographic as Joshua Tree because of sightings, and also new age settlers who ran occult boutiques there offered spiritual tours. The area is also the sacred ancestral lands of the Winnemem Wintu. In a long, brutal list of settler harm, the Shasta Dam continued to be the source of problems in the region. Avery was interested in the accounts of orbs and other UAPs that frequented the area. But as much as he wanted to reconnect with the orbs, doing it there would likely create more problems for the Wintu.

They had enough on their hands with white people tossing around ashes of their dead willy nilly and clogging up sacred rivers with crystals from China. If Avery was being monitored and he drew government military ops there it would be far worse than bringing misguided hippies with burial urns. Avery decided against going. He resolved to find an unexpected spot akin to another vacant roundabout. He needed an understated place to be in touch with his flying phenomena.

The Pyramid Dam on Chumash territory had its own troubles, and Hard Luck Road was a place Avery wanted to see in the rearview mirror. He was ready for Fortune Fold Avenue to call his name. Avery set up his tent and made his way towards the "Pyramid." The Pyramid was cut into the rock in long horizontal swaths that culminated in a peak at the top to create a highway. The grand size of it had a magical draw that emanated across the shimmering lake water when seen through the windshield of a speeding car. Up close and in person, it felt sad to gaze upon. There was no mystical emanation. It was just another industrial misery. Avery's thoughts darted from stolen land to gold rush to present day, mercury-poisoned waters. Even during a visit at sunset, the site had a somber quality, though the mountains and trees were a balm. He returned to the campgrounds feeling a tad better, but on a deep cellular level, still worn out.

Avery longed to return to his initial encounters with the orbs. There was a sense of promise and near horizons when they entered his life. The first and second visits were the purest thing that he had ever experienced, and it had become a global social media event. He'd been on track towards a new career and community. The agents had confused him. Avery needed to be more respectful to the devout UFO enthusiasts who would never even think of firing military grade weapons as a way to say hello. The broader intelligent universe was a global project, and he could not go it alone. It was that particular longing, to be part of a shared community, that made him such an easy mark for the agents, but he wanted to find kindred spirits.

Avery would need to be more specific and careful about the kind of community he connected with next time. Maybe conferences were a good idea; he had been too arrogant before, as if he was above anyone else's response to off-planet life. UFOs belonged to no one, and everyone should be curious. Avery grew pleased that the field lacked experts. Maybe that was for the best. Maybe the UFOs wanted it that way. Total outsiders or bust. Avery would rather land in a field of everyday citizens dressed in silly green costumes over a military outfit. If given a choice, he would choose to never encounter the orbs again rather than be party to a violent response to their arrival. If that made him stupid and also led to his death by their alien hands or lasers or cattle prods, so be it.

Wind and insects offered much needed space to collect himself. Avery sat on his sleeping bag. He thought about breathable barriers, his skin, the tent fabric and the way oxygen permeated the entire forest. Nature was alive and there was no disconnect. Somewhere in the sky above were the orbs that he touched just by virtue of being alive and comprised of vibrating particles in space. He imagined them hovering far above in a triangle formation.

He thought of Sam. She was so convincing. He remembered his panic before he decided to caravan down to the desert and her perfect thoughtful hook. She had gathered road snacks for the trip. He could not turn her down after she had been so thoughtful to gather him snacks. He ignored his animal instincts. Sam had a bag of mandarins, trail mix, coffee, and a twelve pack of Topo Chico. It would not have surprised Avery if those were all items taken from the van cupboard. Sam got road snacks. She did not say from where. She was probably prompted to push him. He did not remember most of their shared car ride. He had a feeling this was consistent with Sam's evasiveness or tendency to entirely ignore intimate questions. Their shared time on the roundabout was only heated when it was regarding the orbs. She was working. He was her job. Avery was ashamed. Why did he ever have a crush on her? Loneliness made him foolish. They should have scrubbed her from his memory, too. He did not need to fill in the blanks. He wanted none of it. Avery needed to scrap whatever residue had dulled his connection to the orbs. The agents were bad people. There was no Sam to rescue or court. He was an assignment in an operation. She was employed to bring him in.

Avery had trouble sleeping. The little princess on a pea had done a poor job of clearing rocks from underneath his sleeping mat and was too cold to deal with it for several hours. After what felt like all night, he grew frustrated enough to pull on his coat, pants, and another layer of socks within the sleeping bag. He padded around for a softer area and moved his bedding accordingly. He felt confined, near-claustrophobic, and stepped outside. He would not be able to fall asleep again. He glanced up. Leaves moved against the dark sky like fractals. Nature's screensaver. The air was fragrant, it was the cleanest smell he had encountered in years. He wanted to bottle it. The sun was far from up, but the moon afforded the night a soft glow. Avery strode towards an overlook he had visited upon arrival. It was there, in the cold dim light, that Avery felt called to return to the roundabout. The insecurity of missing hours and the shame he felt for falling in with agents dissipated. He was raised to be defiant. He needed to stand up for the orbs and prevent them from being turned into villains like they are dramatized in

Hollywood productions. They were not the ones who stole land, erected dams, and poisoned the earth in the name of progress. And maybe they had some ideas how to improve things around here. No! Avery was not going to let it be socially acceptable to fire first and autopsy later. The "weather balloon" trope that dated back to Roswell and military operations needed to be out in the light of day. UFO Pride, bitches! And with that, Avery fell to the forest floor having a seizure.

* * *

Avery was alone inside a shipping container turned office. The posters that depicted an alien with its guts exposed on a metal table, a poor attempt at kitsch, turned his stomach even in memory. Avery saw his car from the window. He made a run for it. As soon as he cleared the first step, a black hood was thrown over his head and he was restrained. He smelled Jay's body soap. He was jabbed with something, maybe Ativan. He came to in another shipping container. Wrists, ankles, neck, and forehead tightly strapped, he was in traction on a surface with tracks that rotated a full 360°. In his peripheral vision he noticed a live feed that seemed to show his heat signature but colorful, like aura photography. He was terrified. High on the wall a screen played a clip from one of Avery's social media videos on a loop. It was from the time the orbs had formed a double triangle above the roundabout. Avery was rotated to face the screen in order to elicit an emotional reaction. He instinctively closed his eyes to resist whatever they wanted from him. He smelled Jay approach.

"Don't fight. We are almost done."

Despite himself, Avery welled up and cried. He felt stupid.

"X and Sam, we did what you are doing right now, but voluntarily, because we took the job. This part was inevitable. It's the program. You are sharing something unique, like a fingerprint. I took the job, so I got paid for mine. You did not take the job, so it's an in-kind gesture, a donation. You will not get paid."

"Donating what? What the hell is this thing?"

"Put simply, we're capturing your vibes. We're documenting the way you transmit and receive remote signals. It's best if you surrender to the process. You're nearly finished, Avery. As long as you don't get too rigid or overly emotional. Then it will take longer. I will need to drug you again."

"Why are you doing this?"

"My job is gathering antennas, people like us who have exchanges with UFOs, to learn how they communicate. We're building a database for research and deployment. We won't need your physical presence once we complete these scans. We can use your unique auric signature in the field to make contact."

A door creaked and slammed open as a gust of wind blasted against the side of the shipping container. The subsequent groan was recognizable. It was Xander.

The machine spun and placed Avery face-to-face with a video of the orbs in a double triangle. He heard his own voice whisper "*You guys,*" then some shuffling, then his voice saying "*Triangle.*" Avery's present emotional state was far from the man in that moment. They wanted him to close the gap, but he was no longer that person and felt resentful. He was unwilling to play along if he could help it.

"I think we got what we needed. Look."

In the silence that followed, Avery guessed some kind of data display was being shown to Xander.

"Maybe."

"They always start to resist around now. Funny, huh?"

"They do, we did. We should find a way to speed it up. Avoid this part."

A different video began on the screen above Avery. He watched as a tear rolled down his face. He heard himself tell his audience that he would remain at the roundabout but needed a minute to gather himself. Xander and Jay watched along, and Avery felt ashamed for being so vulnerable in public.

"Avery's lesbian mommy made him so comfy and in touch with his emotions," Jay cackled to himself, then disappeared.

The traction rotated and Avery was upright. Xander was in Avery's face, his elbow in the air ready to push more drugs into Avery's system with a needle jab. Avery tried to mentally record the room. He wanted to remember what happened. He was rolled from the human hamster wheel, still in restraints, then loaded into an enclosed space like a sensory deprivation tank, or a body temperature, water-lined, roomy coffin. He lost the bounds of his body thanks to the drugs. He was a stick floating in a riverbed. He was the riverbed. He was a formless idea. It was pleasant and calm. Something like a noise concert commenced and he wondered if he would ever see his mother again.

Avery came to on the forest floor with leaves stuck to his face. He shivered uncontrollably and noticed wetness all over his crotch. He had pissed himself. When he stood up it felt like a hammer had bashed his skull. He nearly blacked out, but the darkness receded like an undertow. Avery was cold, confused, and unsure where his tent was planted. Death was his first prayer; his second was knowing the direction of his campsite. It was a particular kind of hell, which made it difficult to know what deity to beg for help. He dialed direct to the whole fucking universe and/or whatever forest spirits were in reach to please guide him back. Or end him right there and then. Avery heard the crack of a twig and followed the sound. Within a few minutes he spotted the outer flanks of the campsite.

Once inside his tent, exhaustion hit. His coat covered in dirt, his pants and long underwear urine soaked, he made a skirt from his towel and thanked heaven for clean dry socks. He used that small blessing as the strength needed to hang the wet clothes on low branches just outside the tent flaps. Avery shivered. He crept into his sleeping bag and decided when the sun appeared he would drive home without stopping.

15

Julia noticed an email from the art program and her stomach dropped. She skimmed the letter, saw the word "unfortunately" and stopped reading. Julia texted Franklin and apologized for not getting accepted. She wanted to do it on her own without his help, but maybe it would have made the difference. She did not say that part, only the apology for being rejected. Julia rolled a joint and went outside. The oak tree was the closet relation she had at the moment, and she hoped to find solace.

She shared the news with the tree and asked if it was okay if she smoked a plant while leaning against its trunk. It seemed like it could be poor etiquette, but the oak was happy for the company. The oak lamented about the drought and shared how it had changed the overall mood of the yard. Wildlife had diminished too. There used to be more birds in the tree branches. Now it was mostly chaotic squirrels with little regard for the oak. Julia continued to feel like sudden telepathy was valuable in the right hands. She did not have those hands or any real relationship to the outdoors. It was wasted on her. The tree observed that Julia could be a quick study with the so-called natural world. The tree thought the concept of nature was silly and preferred to call it *existence*. Julia did not feel like an artist anymore. She was just a girl with a Polaroid camera and a phone. The notion of her having a practice seemed like a joke.

Julia was unable to grasp the schooling on offer from the oak. She never fully recovered from being called a murderer by the front lawn. It was still embarrassing. Regardless, she was able to relax in the backyard and enjoy her friendship with the oak. The oak felt like a one-off. The front yard and all life beyond it still required hiding in her headphones. The hedges were fickle. Each time Julia thought their dynamic had improved she learned it had not. The oak told Julia about crows that used to hang out in the neighborhood. There was a kid who lived next door that threw rocks at the large black birds. He hit one and damaged its wing. Crows descended and the kid ran inside. The crows never forgot that kid's face. Anytime he was outside, and they saw him, it was on. That was the end of the oak's story, but Julia wanted to know what else happened. The tree thought it was fairly obvious that the family moved away. Julia was curious if the tree shared that story because the front yard was never going to forget Julia's involuntary plantslaughter. Was it time to leave Franklin's house? No. The oak suggested Julia replace a few houseplants and care for them as an act of restitution. Julia was not ready to risk it. She was concerned that if she messed up again, she would never be able to show her face in Franklin's neighborhood and would need to move far away just like the family with the baby psychopath.

The tree thought Julia was being dramatic and asked her what she planned to do for work. It was a good question. Julia had money from trimming weed and was not paying any rent. Staying home or blasting music when she left Franklin's yard was not sustainable in the long run. Julia asked the oak tree why the telepathy was happening to her specifically. The tree was uncertain. It did not know if it was spiritual or had any heightened meaning. It was happenstance, as frustrating as that might be. Julia sensed that the hedges were her best bet since they had put it in her head that there was a simple reason why. Julia noticed that the tree's mood had shifted. She was draining it and making things all about herself. The tree was upset about the drought and lack of birds, plus the chaotic squirrels. Julia was not sure what advice to give on that front. She figured it was better to be quiet. She stroked the bark and turned her body to embrace the oak in a tight hug.

* * *

A few hours later in Franklin's kitchen, Julia decided to make a plan to rejoin society, and put a two-week deadline to find a job on the calendar. She never meant to care about her application or assign any meaning to it. Unfortunately, her hopes had been raised and she found that she had really wanted it to happen. Knowing she was going to start art school held the potential to make any job in the meantime temporary, a way to save money while she had free rent. Now any job she took was an actual job, and, thus, the thing she was doing with her life. She did not know what kind of job she could hold down while hearing plants. She might need to move somewhere desolate, blanketed in snow like Antarctica, or an arid desert. The other option was a bustling area where the volume of the city might drown out her telepathy. Art had been a place to transmute her mental health like an alchemist. Plant-telepathy was an artistic goldmine. She had also let herself become very alone. Rejection from the art program sank any visible horizon. Franklin texted Julia that he was sorry for her news. He was proud of her for trying and was there for her if she wanted to talk. He encouraged her to keep making work and said that rejection did not make her any less of an artist. If anything, it made her more of one. Take a moment, dust off and keep going. Eye roll. Julia did not want comfort from him, let alone encouragement or advice. What she wanted now, more than anything in the world, was a dumpster fire emoji to send his way. A tombstone would have to suffice.

If Avery had not been Evil's offspring Julia would have sought him out for sex to fill the void. Julia needed to take the edge off and had accidentally abandoned her sex toys in the throuple van. She had restricted herself from using Evil's book as sexual fodder but no longer needed to worry about being unprofessional. She was no longer Evil's future student. Julia could fantasize about Evil as much as she wanted—finally, the silver-lining. She would not have a career as an artist but could now imagine an affair without being a total creep. The living room seemed like a terrible place to jerk off, and Franklin's bedroom still felt awkward.

Julia decided to take a bath and smoked a bit more. She lit candles, then flipped through Evil's book. The cover image was still her favorite photo. She leaned the book against the wall where she could see it from the tub but far enough away to keep it safe from water damage. Julia created a semi-circle of tea candles to see Evil's face even with all the light fixtures turned off. The ambience was witchy and perfect. Julia gazed at young Evil Fated from afar. It was an altar. A prayer for someone just like that to enter her and her life. A long thick candle flickered and went out. Julia reached for it from the steamy tub and slipped. Hot wax landed on her arm. It hurt in a good way. She washed the candle with soap then pulled it under the water. She rubbed it between her legs until she forgot the book cover and everything else. She wondered if she should penetrate herself with the candle stick, but then worried about a broken piece of dry wax lost in her vag. It was a deal breaker. She rinsed the candle and then ignored it like a bad date. She returned to using her fingers. Julia's eyes drifted over to the empty ceiling hook, and she recalled the hanging plant. Maybe it was time to replace just one.

* * *

The plant nursery was called "The Plant Nursery" and Julia did not want to be there. She could barely cross the parking lot without being overwhelmed. Julia tried to keep her headphones around her neck, but the cacophony of telepathic communication was beyond anything she had ever experienced. She felt like she was going to faint or puke or both. She gave up, pulled on her headphones, and turned back towards the parking lot.

She happened to notice a woman with stringy hair and an ugly green work vest in an argument with a fern. It was clear to Julia that they were having words but no one else noticed. Julia tried to eavesdrop. It was far more advanced than anything she had ever attempted—let alone in public. As she focused on the woman and the fern—they keyed right back into her—an unanticipated two-way street. They shared a look of confusion and then the woman stormed off into the well-manicured greenery. Julia tried to ask the fern if it was okay or needed her help but it was too difficult to single out the fern's telepathic thread in the jumbled surrounds. Julia did not have language for what she was trying to do. The nursery was more complex to tease out than the low-key way she relaxed under the oak. Julia drew nearer to the fern and reached out to touch it. A hand pulled Julia's left headphone away from her ear. Julia smelled coffee and cigarettes.

"You're a nosy one," she said.

"And you're a handsy one," Julia quipped.

The person released her headphone and it snapped against her ear. Julia spun around and read the oval name tag, "Patricia."

She looked into Patricia's eyes and lowered her headphones to give her a piece of her mind. The second the headphones were off, Julia was too overwhelmed and lost her balance.

Patricia grabbed her arm. "Shhhh, focus on your breath. Feel your heartbeat in your chest."

Julia nodded uncertainly. She tried to calm down, then focused on her breath and heartbeat, it worked for a moment. The din of the plant noise made her seasick. Julia thought she was going to puke and ran to the parking lot. The horizon slanted upwards in a diagonal line across her field of vision. She was woozy and lowered herself down to a yellow parking block in an empty space. She put her head between her legs.

Patricia stood before her, "You can't sit there. It's dangerous. A truck bumper will barrel into your head. Do you want that?"

"I just want a second."

"One."

Julia was annoyed but that helped her relax. Her equilibrium returned.

"Why were you arguing with that plant?" Julia stood and cupped her hand against her forehead to see Patricia's face without the sun in her eyes.

"That was a personal matter," Patricia crossed her arms.

"How do you work here with all of this noise?"

Patricia smirked. "I've been receiving for years. I barely remember what you are going through, but I know it when I see it."

"Receiving? Is that just your word or is it, like a thing?"

"Oh, it's a thing. I have to get back. My shift ends at four then I have AA. If you need to talk more, meet me at six in that parking lot across the street—or if you are a friend of Bill, it's a good meeting."

Julia followed Patricia's finger towards a small community center on the far corner of the block.

* * *

The sun set and Julia made her way to the center's parking lot. People trickled out into the area under dim flood lights that flickered. Julia did not expect to see Evil Fated, but she was impossible to miss. A nearby dumpster was a godsend. Julia jumped behind it. It was a long shot, but what if Evil recognized Julia from her application? On top of that it was especially bad timing because she was meeting Patricia of all people. Julia hid in the shadows. She tried to locate Patricia in the small crowd, but it was hard. The lot was sizeable, and she did not see a green vest anywhere. Anonymous strangers in recovery stood around while others disappeared into the night. Julia needed to find Patricia but instead stared at Evil. It was too hard to look away. Evil had aged, sure, but her swagger was sweat inducing. Julia doubled back on her logic and wondered if she should introduce herself. The context of an anonymous meeting that she did not attend made it clear that she had to let it go. She watched from behind the dumpster until Evil left. Julia walked along the sidewalk and stood under a streetlamp. She had given up, but just then Patricia closed the door to the community center. She was the last person to exit.

Julia had mixed emotions about being alone with Patricia and she was unsure why. Patricia waved Julia over to a vintage Chevy truck. Julia balked at the idea of getting in and crafted an excuse. She did not need it. Patricia grabbed a hoodie and shoved something into the glovebox.

"There's a diner up the street. Okay?"

* * *

The Sunspots Diner was near empty and looked exactly like the Double R from *Twin Peaks*. The key difference were the on-theme yellow uniforms and orange checkered floor. Julia and Patricia faced off in red vinyl banquettes. Patricia alternated between coffee, a vanilla shake, and French toast. Julia ate her way through a basket of fries and tried her best to also swallow the information coming at her. Julia found Patricia unsettling at best.

"I used to be a serious person. I had a high-pressure government job and was well-regarded. I was on the brink of transitioning to work in a program at NASA when everything changed. It was during a battery of tests. I had not slept in more than twenty-four hours probably, maybe longer, it's hard to say. There were sensory deprivation studies and ones with varying amounts of oxygen depletion. A psych evaluation was required to proceed to the next level.

I was placed in a room and told to wait there. It was just me and a spider plant in a very simple office space. I rested on the couch. The spider plant made light conversation. I ignored it at first. I was worn down physically and mentally. It was a vulnerable situation and I began to realize that if I could hear the plant, of course others could too. I wondered if there was a tiny speaker, but it did not feel like it was coming from a sound system of any kind. Was the plant *a plant*? Was it actually talking to me? I was at one of the most prestigious government outposts. It made sense that at that level, there was technology that allowed for inter-species exchange. I struggled, because I didn't know if they wanted me to engage with the plant or ignore it. What were the implications if the plant was conducting my psych evaluation and I ignored it? Not a good look, and I wanted to work at NASA. Small talk ended. The plant dropped into a series of profound questions and shared thoughtful responses when I finally gave in. We had a dialogue about some hypothetical scenarios regarding space travel, spirituality, and the cosmos. The plant encouraged me to move towards the more secretive programs that dealt with paranormal phenomena; some had been off the books since the '50s. I was considering the plant's advice and then a man in a suit and horn-rimmed glasses entered with my folder in his hand. He was ready to conduct my psych eval and apologized for running so late."

The fry Julia held onto for the duration of this tale went limp in her fingers. "Holy fucking shit. So then what happened?"

Patricia slurped the bottom of the metal cup that held the extra part of her malted. She was nearly done with her meal.

"Oh hon, we have to skip ahead. Long story short, I drank my way through the next decade to cope. I was Type A and compartmentalized up to a point. Let's just say that our government has a violent underbelly that is charged with the task of eliminating any life that endangers the power of who it was built to serve—terrestrial or extra-terrestrial. I quit my very serious life. I got sober. I admitted to myself that I was a telepathic receiver. I saw what happened to other telepathic receivers, antennas and the like—most sent to psych wards, cages, penniless on the streets at best. I needed to be somewhere safe. Working with plants and talking to them is my job. I keep a low profile. Every year, more and more newbies like you show up. The plants say that it is a critical moment. They are getting louder and taking more risks, in my opinion. So now, even someone like you can hear them."

"Someone like me?" Julia inquired. She did not like Patricia's tone, which had suddenly become harsh.

"You seem like a horny slut who never had to work too hard. Good teeth. Nice tits. You should keep your pretty mouth shut. You don't want to get sent to a mental ward or thrown in a cage, do ya? See how easily you confided in me about being a photosympathizer? This country loves locking people up. Well, don't get me locked up."

Patricia chewed on her straw having polished off the last of her order. She leaned back and met Julia's gaze with a hardened stare. "Don't come back to my work. And if you are a smart woman that I have accidentally misjudged as a horny slut, don't advertise, don't attract attention, fly under the radar, okay? Control your shit. Be subtle. Don't engage too much with the plants and mostly, shut the fuck up about it. We don't need the government in our business. It is nobody's business. No one needs to know about it. Keep it to yourself. And don't you talk to Fern again or even ever look at her again! And if you try to touch her delicate fronds ever again—I will do things you can't even imagine. You don't want to know what I know how to do!"

She was right. Julia definitely did not want to know. She slid across the vinyl so fast it burned her legs. Wallet in hand she darted towards the server, "I need to pay the bill. Please."

The server bopped to the register. Julia was overwhelmed. She stared at a glass cake stand with oatmeal cookies on an oily paper doily by the register. Julia turned for a split second and watched as Patricia commandeered the rest of her fries.

The server spoke softly, "Her bark is worse than her bite. She always ends her meals with barbs, does it with our staff, too. She lures people in and then burns bridges to cut them loose twice as fast. I have never seen her here with the same person twice. And I have rarely seen her pay for a meal. It's a game. Don't take it personally, sweetie. Save your tears."

Julia nodded. She blinked away the tears that had just started to form. She paid the check and walked swiftly to the door.

Patricia called after her, "Hey, Julie! Julie, you know why I come here? Because sunspots block transmissions and signals. All of them. Very relaxing. Very quiet. You should try their breakfast combo."

Julia waved goodbye and left before any tears went public. She was embarrassed and scared that she was in the throes of a mental breakdown. And that Patricia was a sneak preview of her future self. She unlocked her phone to dial Reggie but saw the updated contact name she had made for such an occasion—*Do NOT Call Reggie*— and it stopped her. She looked at her phone for directions back to Franklin's. It was walkable and any additional time and space offered a psychic cleanse. Julia's dark chaotic energy was not something she wanted to bring home. She needed to stop crying so she put on an upbeat playlist.

Julia paused at the plant nursery. It was dark and locked shut with a single chain on the fence that looked easy to scale. She wondered what Patricia would do if she stole the fern. Or worse, if she got another employee to sell the fern to her? It was probably a bad move. Julia felt broken, her hopes dashed. She wanted to lash out. Patricia was a confusing disappointment. It was hard to know if she was a reliable narrator or out of her mind. Julia approached the center of the parking lot. She contemplated her need for more drama in her life. Did she need to poke the bear in a tin foil hat? No, she did not. Along the way home, Julia put keywords that included "receiver" and "antenna" into a search engine. A/V equipment and ads appeared. The term "telepathy" was a fast track to nowhere and also to films from the '80s and '90s, UFO conspiracy websites, and something trending about teenage cat psychics. She wished she could confide in someone reliable to make sense of why this was happening to her.

Four songs later, Julia learned that she had forgotten to leave a light on, but streetlamps helped. She rounded the hedges a little too quickly and brushed against firm leaves with her arm. She turned and apologized as she made her way to the porch. She fumbled with the key in the dark and slid her hand along the wall until she found the light switch. Julia shut the door and removed her headphones. She was lonely. The couch beckoned her like the unconditional embrace of a grandmother.

* * *

Julia's heart raced. There was an email from Evil Fated Studio in her inbox, "Hi Julia, if you have any interest in a studio assistant position, please give me a call. Enjoyed your essays and photography.—E." Julia pinched herself and the email still existed, right in front of her eyes. Julia ran to the bathroom. She splashed water on her face, fixed her hair, and put on lipstick. She took two long breaths on her way back to the couch and dropped her shoulders. Julia dialed the number. It rang twice. Julia was unprepared for voicemail, but Evil answered on the third ring.

"Evil, umm … Hey, I got your email, it's Julia."

"Hi Julia. Sorry you didn't get into the program."

"That's okay."

"I need to hire an assistant and you expressed an interest in working with me in your essay."

"I did. I do … have an interest in that."

"Cool. Do you want to come by the studio on Monday around noon to see if it's a good fit? The address is in the email."

"Yes. I see it. Okay, Monday at noon."

Julia wanted to keep the conversation going but was too amped to say anything sensible. It felt huge to see the studio even if it was not a fit. A fit would be better. She had to seem professional and not stupid. She felt stupid for not being picked for the program and she did not want to be a pity hire, but at least it was Evil's idea. It was unprompted and out of nowhere, like a sexy miracle. Julia needed to become more cultured immediately. She only had a few days. It would not be the first time she had hijacked Franklin's well-curated queer archives. He did the hard yards and she got to indulge with ease. Plus, she had the benefit of the internet.

She returned to Evil's book and cross-referenced her portrait subjects with the internet. Whenever she landed on an artist, she read up on them. If they were still alive, she would look to see what they were doing at present. Many were dead, a good number from AIDS complications. Ronald Reagan was a real piece of shit, she thought. The more she read, the more she felt like she was living in a bad spin-off, many of the same bad actors appeared in both shows.

Julia had gone to protests, but only encountered a Pride parade once. She found it oddly demoralizing. There were rainbow balloon floats, cops, and corporate employees dressed in respective logo t-shirts tucked into khakis. "YMCA" played on a loop. If Citizens United made corporations people, the Pride parade was them coming out briefly and then going back into the closet for eleven months. It was saccharine, an oversaturated reproduction of gay culture that made her feel embarrassed by the notion of "visibility," if that is what people saw when they looked at gay. Her intense private shame, combined with gratitude for all the people who fought to make Pride a thing regardless of its trappings, made her sure that she was at least a little bit gayer than she had initially thought.

Regardless, identity had little to do with her life. She was not big into identifying as anything in particular. She had no real pride and felt meaningless. Patricia from the nursery nailed it when she called her a horny slut. Reggie loved any queer gathering and identified as a bisexual lesbian. It was a confusing label that Julia let wash over her rather than ask a few simple questions. In the end, Reggie would not cut out the middleman, so Julia came to find that Reggie knew herself well and was upfront about it. Perhaps Julia would have benefited from listening when Reggie told her who she was, but would it have mattered? Julia was not a monogamous lesbian who had been betrayed. She was just a horny slut who should have insisted on a limited run of three-ways rather than throupling up.

Sexual tension mounted as Julia perused hot homosexuals in Evil's photo work. It really did a number on her. She needed to go clear her head or find a bar or someone on an app. She did not want anyone in Franklin's house. There were no nearby lesbian spaces she knew about. She decided to just go to the closest watering hole.

The bar within walking distance was lackluster. The Happy Hour crowd had thinned out to a despondent moment. Two bartenders looked bored. One of them was cute and seemed to only be a few years older than Julia. She flirted with him as she ordered the mezcal drink special. He had thick glasses, short curly hair, a thick well-groomed beard, and septum ring. He wore a black Joy Division *Unknown Pleasures* muscle tee. She figured he would smell like jaunty men's soap and artisan beard oil. She cut to the chase, ready to return to her arts and culture cram session back home.

She leaned towards him. "Are you single and ready to mingle with me?"

"What do you mean?"

He was dull. Julia wanted sex to fall in her lap as it should. His eyes were glued to her cleavage—*what did she mean*? Please. She shrugged and spun away on the barstool. She scanned the room for lower hanging fruit and finished her drink. The bartender was suddenly in her ear with a resounding, "Yes." More like it.

They faced each other in a back office the size of a broom closet that doubled as a broom closet. It smelled like orange-scented cleaner that was more chemical-heavy than fragrant. She leaned into his chest to inhale clean dude smell and instead discovered funky body odor rather than palo santo as hoped. Julia did not want to smell like him at all. She reached her hand out then stroked him over his jeans, a gap between them. He flipped up her skirt, tucked it into the waist then moved her underwear to the side in one swift move. Julia had two thoughts, first, she was glad she had trimmed her bush because it looked hot, and second, she would cop his technique when she next had the chance. Then, not to be outdone, she reciprocated by releasing the button on his jeans and zipper in an equally seamless choreography. They both got hard and finished without using more than hands. It was quick. Julia felt like they both entered a state of play that required little more than physical contact and decent imagination.

He cleaned up using a bar towel and asked if she would stick around for another drink. Julia shook her head. The bartender chuck-led like he figured as much. Julia left the bar feeling more relaxed but lonely. At least she had spiced up self-pleasure with someone else's fingers and moved another step away from Reggie.

On the way home Julia was in a bind. She'd headed to the bar in a thirsty trance. She did not have the right bag for her look, and had left the house with an ID, housekey, and cash tucked in her boot. Without her phone it was impossible to ignore the local flora. Lawns cried out, "Bring out your dead!" as she passed compost bins on garbage night. Julia felt seasick for the first time since the nursery. She focused on her breath and heartbeat. It did not do much of anything, stupid Patricia probably just made it up to get rid of her and get a free meal. Julia was only a few blocks from Franklin's when she experienced an overwhelming gravitational pull to sit on the ground. Pinpricks of light shot across her eyes followed by a plummeting sadness that made her stomach drop. She noticed a pine tree across the street and decided to will herself towards it. She blacked out and came to holding onto the tree. She had no memory of the time between where she had stood and the tree. It was a great relief that she did not get hit by a car or bash into a mailbox.

The pine tree was a safe place to land. She felt the earth rotate on its axis and there was still a bit of a battle to stay upright. She focused on the tree's energy and fell against its trunk. She became closed off to all other stimuli and tried to connect with the pine. She needed to know why she felt so horrible. Why was this happening?

The pine was hearty and warm. It was not long before she felt soothed and held. The pine was less chatty than the oak tree that she had come to know well, but it calmed her in a way that so few in her life had ever been able to. Julia lowered down onto the roots and focused on the texture of the bark. It was flat and built up by many uneven layers. She prayed that no one would stop to ask why she was laying on the ground like that. She sensed the tree's consideration of her questions. It had a digestive quality to it, thorough contemplation and then some.

In the pine's humble o'piñon, the question itself was an issue. The tree did not have answers for it, but shared the wisdom that it was best to meet life where it was. For example, when the tree was just a sapling there was no sidewalk surrounding it. Years later, as a full-grown tree, not only was there a sidewalk, but black asphalt. The pine was upset for decades, anguished even, and as the area became more developed and heavily landscaped, the tree could either stay stuck in the past or accept its current circumstances. The tree made peace with the sidewalk and lived a well-connected life underground which helped the pine ignore the stupid cement. A bustling social scene took root because of all the plantings and one fine day, the tree was part of a growing effort to crack the sidewalk in three places. It was only a matter of time. The tree recommended making the most with what she had in the meantime. Tough love or bust. The tree's best guess was that her lack of self-acceptance made her seasick. Julia fought her nature because telepathy was too hard to reconcile. The tree did not want to needle her about it. She needed to establish a new equilibrium and own her gift. At least she was not the kind of psychic that got yelled at and haunted by ghosts! That was true. Hounded by hedges was far better.

Julia was impressed with how grounded the tree seemed to be. Its tremendous presence was stable and solid. Julia could barely deal with herself and her observations. Her inner thoughts sounded like someone on hallucinogenic drugs for the first time. She wanted to handle her shit. The tree made sense and helped her. There was no point in resisting who she was, and if she did, it would make her unwell. Telepathy felt more manageable, but the seasickness-overwhelm was hard to take. Julia still felt if she knew why this had happened to her, it would be useful in knowing what to do with it. The pine disagreed and grew crestfallen. The tree did not like it when its hard-won wisdom seemed up for debate. It threw up its branches and felt done with her. Mostly the pine was tired of Julia's emotional mulling. She sensed the pine bristle. The sensation was distinctly the opposite of the oak in the backyard who processed with her at length.

She could not help her thought cycle. Julia was exhausted and sad. She felt truly lost. Her parents were dead. She failed her half-brother by not getting into the art program. Her ex-girlfriend was probably going to marry and have a baby with their third. The bar-tender was cute but smelled like onions. Julia's thoughts slowed and she cried. The pine absorbed her tears, her pain, and offered some comfort. The tree did not like to process but found her emotional release to be far more productive than running mental laps. Despite having plenty of time, the pine did not have time for that. The tree welcomed her darkest emotions and drew them down into the goth party in the depths below, where they would become nitrogen.

16

Evil swept her studio. She wanted to create an impression of cleanliness and order for herself as well for her new potential hire. She hoped to project an aura of professionalism to start on solid footing. It had been years since her last studio assistant and that had ended poorly because the person was a mess. Evil decided to handle all of her business from then on, and that left little time to create work. She emptied the dustpan at the same moment Julia buzzed. She was right on time, which felt like a good sign, but Evil became uneasy when she opened the door.

Julia was far more attractive than the self-portraits in her application, objectively so, and Evil felt an intense physical draw. She was young, coated with a light sweat, and completely magnetic. Also, Julia was not a great actor. She looked at Evil longingly despite her will to appear totally professional. There was an intimacy that already existed between the pair because Evil read Julia's personal essay as well as saw her work. Julia had done her Evil homework and then some. In a word, it was weird. Julia felt too young and stupid. Evil felt too old. Julia laughed and Evil joined in and then they shook hands like jocks or businessmen, each unclear what the other was thinking. Both assumed the worst.

After asking for a glass of water to quench her thirst from her walk to the studio, Julia mentioned how appreciative she was to be considered for the position. She shared how disappointing it was to get rejected from the art program but that she still felt like she got the prize. Evil reassured Julia that she was a real contender and that it was incredibly competitive. The faculty recognized Julia's promise as an artist, and with a bit more on her resume, her application would be stronger for the next time around. Evil doubled down to say that she was really impressed by Julia's work and writing. It inspired Evil to ask her about the studio assistant job. Julia was gracious. She was uncertain how long she would be sticking around town, but if the gig worked out it was reason enough to hang her hat. As soon as Julia mentioned leaving if it did not work out, Evil became subconsciously hooked. Julia was nervous and reminded Evil that there was going to be a learning curve. She really did not know her way around real cameras or lenses.

Julia relaxed at the sight of the long worktable with a laptop on it. "That said, I'm a quick study. All the studio correspondence and social media stuff are a cake walk. This is wild. Being in your studio is a dream." Evil was flattered.

Camera manuals and photography books lined the lowest shelves on a tall metal bookcase. Evil crawled around on the floor, retrieved important technical texts, and made a bundle for Julia to review as homework. She showed Julia the proper way to clean, change, and stow a lens. Julia asked questions about the things she had only been doing intuitively as far as lens size and focal distance. She helped Evil commit to a social media schedule and made a plan to post works from her archive. The decades that separated them made for a fascinating feedback loop. It was dark outside before either noticed how many hours had passed. Time really did get away from them.

Julia was committed to being a good studio assistant, which was not a far-off commitment from her willingness to be a good bottom. Her thinking progressively warped. It was also why she had no clue how long they had been talking. She *wanted* a mentor, but she also wanted her mentor. Julia couldn't stop herself from speaking candidly. "If you ever want to tie me up, pierce or cut me or whatever, I'm totally game." Evil was confused. "Wait, what?"

Julia's face flushed. Her internal organs collapsed but she kept talking. "Like a body, you know, a model or, what's it called, a stand-in? I don't know your process. I mean, I've seen your work, obviously, and so like for a shoot, if you ever needed that? I'm happy to be that. Is it weird or an overstep to offer something like that? So awkward. I did not mean to make it all weird, but it seems like I did. I wanted to … please, never mind." Evil nodded. It was uncomfortable but also made sense. Evil guessed it was good to know but did not say so. Evil yawned. She stood up to suggest that was that. Time to go. Julia was scared she was not hired or already fired. She pushed it—she deserved to be tossed out—but then Evil smiled. "I look forward to your assistance in a few days. I will get some archival things organized in the meantime."

Julia exhaled as she exited Evil's studio. She was unsure if she could be fully professional with someone so hot. She had her headphones on but did not get too far away before a patch of irises got her attention. She could not understand what they were trying to communicate. She nervously lowered her headphones, and a strange psychic feeling passed through her. Julia spontaneously knew that she had forgotten the bundle of books that Evil had worked so hard to gather. She was uncertain if the irises had just helped her realize that somehow. She ran back to the studio and arrived right as Evil opened the door to lock up. Her hand was on the light switch.

"Forgot the books!" Julia brushed past Evil, and she raced over to the table.

Evil offered her a ride home when she saw Julia with full arms. Julia smiled. "If it really isn't a hassle, I would love a ride."

* * *

Julia made sure to seem surprised when Evil suggested they were practically neighbors. She simply nodded and tried to widen her eyes to feign surprise. She stopped breathing when Evil said her place was merely a "stone's throw" from Julia's. Julia wanted to be thrown. She stared at Evil's tattooed hands, willing them towards her; clearly it was meant to be. EVIL FATE on her knuckles, daggers on her thumbs. Julia wondered what it would be like to have a fist full of evil inside of her, or what about fate? Julia could not remember if Evil was left or right-handed. She had not paid attention. Evil cleared her throat. Julia startled back to the present moment, the one in which Evil was an actual person waiting for her to get out of her car. Julia laughed since there was nothing else to do and Evil laughed too. Evil did not know what the hell was going on with the kid, but she was definitely intriguing. Julia chirped, "Goodnight," as she closed the car door and then kept her eyes on the curb.

The hedges made exaggerated kissing noises. Julia asked them to stop it. "Why are you always up in my business?" Julia went inside and spilled her book bundle on the floor by the coffee table. She felt like she should celebrate with a beer which was unusual. She grabbed a cold IPA from the fridge and went out to the backyard. "You would not believe my day." She hugged then kissed the bark of the oak tree and sat with her back against the trunk. She drank her beer and stroked the roots with her opposite hand. Julia pictured the studio and replayed little moments in her mind's eye. The oak was inside the memory with Julia, able to receive the most vivid and palpable parts. The tree was sorry that Julia did not get accepted into the program, but thought it was good that the institution would no longer be implicated in her tawdry fantasies. Julia countered that she planned to be super professional. It was just an art crush, and once they spent more time together in a workplace setting her lust would die down. The tree suggested that Julia should date someone proactively. Otherwise, it would be a story as old as time. The oak was adamant. Julia hoped if she made herself sexually available, Evil might not pass it up just because she was partnered, maybe they were open. The oak dug in—there was a fifty percent chance Evil would okay it with her partner, or a fifty percent chance she would cheat on her partner. The prospect that nothing would happen was zero percent. The oak was unwavering. Julia did not agree. She explained that when she accidentally flirted it went south like a verbal car crash, complete with a horrible scraping sound on the pavement, not just plain terrible, but sprinkled with awful. Julia was mortified and it was not a feeling she ever wanted to relive. Therefore, she was not going to flirt with Evil again. Sure, she may stare a little too long or pine over her privately just a tiny bit. But her feelings would be a private obsession at most. Then Julia cooed, "I think her nipples are pierced."

17

Evil dabbed blood from Julia's chest with a soft cloth. She wore black latex gloves and set a tray of needles down on the stool next to the one where Julia was bound. Julia arched her back and repositioned herself so that Evil's fingers grazed her nipple with plausible deniability. Julia's immediate arousal betrayed the ruse. Julia did not want to sublimate any longer. She needed to be fucked or admonished, a win-win aside from perhaps losing her job. Evil gave nothing away and continued to clean Julia's chest. Julia pressed into the cloth strokes and exhaled nearly inaudible sighs. The blood was mostly gone but Evil continued her efforts, unable to help herself. It was intoxicating. She could have untied Julia's hands sooner. Presumably they were done with the shoot. Evil finally stopped her little game and released Julia's appendages from the rope.

"You okay?"

Julia was not. She relocated Evil's gloved hand and placed it between her legs.

"No. Can you please do something about this?" she asked with a desperation that made Evil lose her mind.

Evil's hand slid inside Julia. Julia wrapped her arms around Evil and embraced her new role as a hand puppet. They moved to the long wooden worktable. "Will you sign a consent form?"

"I will sign anything you want me to, in blood, just don't stop."

* * *

Catherine traveled for work all of the time. When she was not traveling, she scheduled every free moment and would have taken calls in her sleep if that was an option. She was pleased that Evil was back in the studio but noticed something heightened about her energy. On her way to the airport, Catherine decided something was off and called to ask about her assistant. Evil knew Catherine's time was short. It was best to give the headline and not bury the lead. She explained that Julia's offer to model or help be a canvas for ideas made Evil feel confused, despite its potential usefulness. Catherine took this to mean it would help Evil's work to play with Julia's body and have sex with her. Catherine told Evil not to make herself legally vulnerable.

Not long after the call, Catherine sent Evil an HR agreement for sexual consent along with the releases she needed to cover her ass in all the ways. Catherine thought she might ice the secret affair and perhaps even kill it in its tracks by being forensic. She also tried to be okay with it and said if Julia made the first move and they had sex once, Evil could have a get out of jail free card without any need to ever discuss it. But she better not let it get out of hand, and Catherine wanted to be in the loop if it did. The only power she chose to exercise was to try to make it boring and uneventful. Catherine had not met Julia and did not think she would make a first move. If she bravely made such a pass, young Julia should be rewarded for her effort in seducing an iconic leather dyke. In Catherine's mind, the affair would never last and also might be worthwhile, if strong new work came out of it. Evil seemed shut down because of Catherine's recent success and was creatively blocked. If Catherine was wrong and lost Evil, so be it. She loved her partner, but she had a very full plate. Her career had never existed at this clip and major institutions were offering her serious money to curate artists that she long admired, in addition to running her own gallery. She suspected there might be an emergent mental health crisis afoot, possibly stress-related given that plants were now talking to her, but so far, she had out-paced all that with no plans to stop.

* * *

Julia had decided being fisted by Evil was worth any possible consequence. She no longer cared about art or photography or having a mentor. The opportunity to have been a studio assistant had been thrilling. She was twenty-five and given the amount of PFAs in everything, cancer seemed inevitable, plus sea level rise, there was nothing to lose by living in the moment. She longed to put her body in Evil's hands, to be embraced and placed upon a surface where she would be mauled. Julia was ready to be wrung out like a mop. A mop that would then be used to clean the studio floors and then spanked for doing a bad job as a bad mop. Really nothing else mattered outside of that.

After being pierced and photographed, the prospect of being Evil's bottom outweighed everything else on the planet. Julia's thoughts continually returned to her desire to be consumed by Evil, destroyed even. Evil was not oblivious. Things had shifted between them after the physical contact. It was heated the moment Evil pierced Julia's skin. She pierced and photographed Julia as a way to explore some older work in the present. She was working something out, and that something might double as a late mid-life crisis. Carnal pleasure was her milieu, and once body fluids flowed it was hard to close the faucet. Evil was in the throes of learning how to open up to desire but not be at its mercy. She was also wary about parroting her older projects. She did not want to reclaim former glory. She wanted to use former practices to turn towards the future and locate something fresh. Sexual energy had always been part of her process, but she never thought young Julia would make an actual move.

She was embarrassed by the sexual consent form Catherine had sent along with other work releases. The documents seemed too real, set to warn her away from acting on her unspoken fantasies. She was shocked to need it. Evil swapped hands and continued to play with Julia. She used her teeth to dislodge a glove. She grabbed the tablet, clicked to her email, and downloaded the consent form. Julia took the tablet, signed the document and then on a whim, opened the camera app. She took a picture of Evil reaching inside of her. Unhappy with the composition, she deleted it. Julia adjusted her legs, placed Evil's other hand on her stomach as a foreground element and snapped a picture. She slid the tablet away and focused all her attention on Evil. Evil had not fucked someone so limber in a long time. She put her mouth where her hands had been, rested Julia's thighs on her shoulders and stood. Julia lay suspended upside down and against Evil's frame. She gripped the table for balance and to keep a shred of sanity. She felt like a kabob on a skewer, like spin art, like a bottle of ketchup spurting onto a plate with a tight squeeze.

* * *

Julia remained shirtless but wore her cut-off shorts on the studio couch. It was certainly some version of business casual. She worked on a list of posts for the social media account. Evil sat at the table and toggled through images from their photoshoot. She was distracted and wanted another excuse to put her hands on Julia. Evil grabbed a smaller digital camera and took Julia's picture. Neither one wanted to work. Evil was the boss and the top. Julia focused on work until Evil repositioned her body and removed her shorts. Evil put down the camera and picked up Julia. They had sex on the studio couch until night fell, and then Evil drove her home.

18

Evil played Alice Coltrane on vinyl and eased into her morning feeling lighter than any time in recent memory. The house was hers and so was the fresh pot of coffee. Before bed she'd reconnected with longtime artist friends who had commissioned her to do a photoshoot of their performance in a forest a few hours away. The job had been scheduled months prior on a work calendar that failed to sync, a random technical glitch that made the call a surprise, but Evil kept that to herself. Their call was pure excitement and logistics. Evil decided it was a divine hand prodding her to refocus the blurry relationship with Julia back towards professional photography and away from recent exploits. It would be easy enough to titrate their connection back down to professional interactions in the field while documenting a legendary Ecosexual artist performance. It did not have to feel like last call with harsh lighting and bad music to foist them back to real life. This was a far better arrangement, organic even. Evil phoned Julia and added oat milk to her coffee. She was ready to leave a message, but Julia answered.

Evil launched in, "I know it doesn't fall on our usual workday, but I was wondering if you would be up for assisting me with a photoshoot tomorrow? I forgot about it because of a calendar mishap. Apologies for the short notice."

"That's okay. What time should I be at your studio?"

"I can come get you because we're actually going to the woods to document an Ecosexual performance piece!"

"Oh. I can't be in the woods."

"You can't be in the woods?"

"Right. It's a health thing."

"What kind of a health thing?"

"Are you asking as my employer or …?" Julia's tone was cold.

"You know, I always planned to do the shoot myself. Not a problem, really. I thought it would be fun. No sweat."

There was a moment of silence on the line. They had only talked to each other on the phone once and that was a brief exchange. Evil did not know if it was a generational divide, but it was uncomfortable.

Julia was quiet but still there. Evil's brain sputtered. She had to cut and run.

"Okay. Thanks. Talk soon."

Evil hung up and pushed the phone away from her. She felt strange. She needed to process.

* * *

It was an hour before Catherine was able to return her call from an antiquated hotel lobby powder room. Catherine was seated on a leather pouf in a dimly lit room of vanity mirrors. The lighting defeated the room's whole purpose. She watched her reflection as they spoke and strained to fix her lipstick. She thought about how gazing into the mirror was similar to her video calls. Part of her brain was present for the information, while another part fixated on her appearance—a familiar neural pathway lit up. She told all of this to Evil at the outset and set a stage for their conversation.

"I am in a room full of mirrors and reflections."

Catherine sounded the way she did when she was not getting enough rest, poetic and philosophical with a caustic edge. Evil aware that consulting her partner to understand another woman was more of a first idea than a best idea, but Catherine's even keel was a foot bridge she desperately needed to cross the currents. They caught up for a bit until Catherine asked how her work was going. Evil shared her calendar mishap but her thrill to see their mutual friends and document their latest piece. She went on to say that something weird happened with her assistant Julia. She asked Catherine if she was aware of any health conditions that prevented someone from being in the woods.

Catherine laughed. "Like what do you mean, allergies?"

Evil offered that if it were allergies, there were over-the-counter medications she could take. She was confused. Catherine asked for the exact conversation to parse out what was going on. Evil recounted their exchange verbatim. Catherine asked if anything sexual had happened since Evil's confirmation that Julia had signed the consent form. Just that time. Catherine was not thrilled, but had to let it go, given her stated boundaries. That process would be easier if the situation was contained, but their conversation made it seem like it was not. What would motivate Julia to forgo the experience of being in the woods with Evil?

Catherine pondered aloud, "Well, maybe she thought you called to get her to come to your studio for sex and was disappointed when it was actually about work, so she said the first thing that came to mind. Were you clear with her about it being a one-off and did you hold that boundary?"

"Yes," Evil lied.

Catherine responded at face value. "You'll need to figure out if working with someone who can't be in the woods is a deal breaker for an assistant. If so, you'll need to let her know that and find another one."

Evil could feel Catherine lower the curtains on the call and imagined her sitting there, feeling self-satisfied with her advice while she gazed at her beautiful echo in the many mirrors. In reality, Catherine felt old and tired, wondered about getting her eyes done. Her feelings changed about the dark powder room and the welcome reprieve delicate lighting afforded as her thoughts drifted to the supple skin of a twenty-five-year-old.

* * *

After Evil and Julia had had sex in the studio, Evil dropped her at home. Around midnight, Evil sent a "you up" text, and fifteen minutes later Julia was astride Evil in her bed. And as Evil imagined would be the case, Julia's eyes were locked on the portrait of young Evil above the bed, like so many of her past lovers, only in this case it was mentorship. The pair tore through the new toys Evil had bought for Catherine but failed to use. Evil spontaneously decided to use new toys only to keep some kind of line in place, despite how slippery everything had gotten. Julia declared that she was fully dehydrated and felt like the aftermath of an all-you-can-eat-buffet plate, in a good way. She demanded to have her walk of shame home as the sun rose. Unless Evil was willing to bind her with duct tape, stuff her in a duffle bag, drive her home in a duffle bag, leave the duffle on the porch and then watch from her car to see if Julia could escape. Evil did not consider the duffle bag. She told her to walk home and that she would watch from the window. The light of day had reified that Julia was in Catherine's bed. Being at the house and having a sleepover was *the* definition of out of hand.

Evil washed the bedding and agonized over the sex toys as soon as Julia shut the door. The motorcycle butt plug was a disappointment because it turned out to be a prostate massager. Evil still had fun using it for a brief puppet show wherein the motorcycle v'roomed along the crevice of Julia's perfect ass. Evil's agony was not that some toys were better than others, but that she could not introduce the newly used toys to Catherine at all. She even had to stop herself from offering them to Julia just because she didn't want them to go to waste. Evil sanitized the toys, put them in a box, wrote "props" across it in marker, and set them by the door to take to the studio.

* * *

As Evil drove Avery's car into the trailhead parking lot, she wondered again, what kind of health thing would prevent someone from being able to be in the woods? Evil had no clue. The woods were healing. They were healthy and natural. Evil wondered if Catherine was right and she had simply let Julia down by offering a work opportunity sans sexual designs. Evil unloaded minimal equipment, two backpacks and a tripod. Her arrival was perfectly timed to trail a gaggle of young artists in scant attire to the project site. Evil greeted her friends and received kisses. She was told it would be a concupiscent atmosphere and they needed her to participate. Despite requesting her presence as the photographer, they wanted Evil to wear a costume. The green pleather harness and pants reminded her of Lederhosen. She knew better than to fight the mood. Evil found a thick tree trunk to change behind. She did not know where her shyness came from but chalked it up to the creeping vulnerability she had felt since her call with Julia. At least Julia was not there for the elfin wear.

Evil photographed ambiguously gendered artists as they glued flowers to each other's nipples. She took close-ups of jock straps refashioned into Venus fly traps. The fly traps were placed on the forest floor and worn by artists to suggest a sexual equivalency between all life forms. The performance was infectious, joyous, and visceral. Evil was the recipient of lusty glances from a heavily-inked trans femme with a serious mullet, and another youngish artist with a bowl cut. The two of them put effort into being photographed by Evil, gave their best angles and eyes while still being present in the performance. Evil was attracted to both and unsure which one she preferred. Sexual energy was sticky, like pollen or mushroom spores hitching a ride. She was covered in it and so was everyone else. Evil was Pan in green pleather.

Evil had not intended to attend the afterparty at the motel. She was caught up in the moment and unable to part ways, so she traveled in the caravan. The animal unleashed by Julia had no plans to be tamed back into its well-behaved cage. She needed to be where the hot queers were romping about. Artists skinny-dipped in the pool until a family complained to the motel's registration office. The party moved between four rooms. Evil used her smaller camera and played voyeur. Wigs and drugs and booze and artists that longed to be photographed made for a playful evening. They all knew who Evil was and secretly would have killed to be in the situation they now found themselves. The vibe remained nonchalant, betrayed by rolling waves of attention-seeking. It was hard to say if it was the molly or the LSD that turned the room into an improv theater photoshoot, or if it was destined to happen by nature of the people present. It did not take long for all of Evil's equipment to relocate from inside her car.

Evil remained behind the tripod as a group of ten artists took turns in front of her lens. They performed in staged scenes the others devised. It was like a hive of bees in a dance-off, and then in a flash the relevant props were thrown onto the bed. Staged photos of break-ups, treachery, lurid affairs, and artistically rendered body piles carried on for hours. Evil did not remember when she decided that it was okay for her to take molly and half a hit of LSD. Her consideration was brief, given the way her brain had already run the obstacle course like a pre-crime. All that recent talk of therapeutic trials, creative breakthroughs, micro-dosing success stories, the history of AA and psychedelics, and California sobriety had relaxed unnoticed in a hammock slung across her brain stem until someone finally offered her something in a way that seemed okay. Had Evil only said yes to the small amount of LSD it would have been low-key justified in some obtuse logical workaround. The molly absolutely inched beyond those same gates. Evil made a choice even if she did not remember making it. A hotel room full of hot party people was outlandishly far from a therapist's office, a hospital-monitored ketamine drip, or participation in a regimented MDMA research trial. All reasons and questionable decisions aside, Evil felt more alive, felt more of everything, than she had in years. She promised herself she was never going to be a stick in the mud again. She freed her metaphorical stick from dubious suction with a great heave-ho.

The walls around Evil were elastic with breath. They expanded and contracted on all sides, perilously closing in as the entire motel room, floor to ceiling, moaned with pleasure. Evil was in a double bed with Mullet and Bowl Cut, both dressed like Merpeople, one on each of her breasts sucking on her nipples. It was dark aside from a lamp with a tie-dyed indigo scarf thrown over its shade. In the watery light Evil looked down and discovered that she was only dressed in a strap-on with an unfamiliar tentacular dildo. Mullet continuously stroked her long silicone organ. Evil had followed her seafaring friends where the evening called. She'd sobered up a touch or was beyond the peak, because she had enough awareness to choose if she wanted to pull herself together or follow through with her compulsion to play with their sexy butts. She opted for the latter and had some of the weirdest sex she had had in her entire life, an alien-mermaid-octopus insemination game with lubricated silicone eggs. It was fun. Herstorically speaking, she was a stone butch top, but the forest spirits snuck inside her every orifice with wild tongues, digits, and dick play. It was unclear when they all found their way into the outdoor hot tub or when the bag of oranges entered the scene.

In some early dawn hour Evil went from hot tub to cold plunge to truly sober up. She wanted to take off before her longtime friends woke up. She did not want her close friends to see her dilated pupils or know how long she had stuck around. While they helped Evil pack up and load her car, she learned that her sensuous new friends were from the Bay Area. Before she left, they followed Evil's social media accounts and insisted she follow them back. Evil gave them money for the motel room and thanked them for an other-worldly adventure. She felt expansive, like her pilot light was back on and she had not even realized it was out. She had been tired for so long that she thought it was her age. It was not.

* * *

Evil pulled up at her house without remembering the drive home. It was unnerving but she was still joyful. She unloaded her car and made coffee. After the shower, her pupils were finally smaller and less dilated. The molly and sex continued to cuddle her warmly in a soft after-glow. A text from Julia appeared on her phone. She needed to explain some things. Could Evil come by?

* * *

Evil arrived at Julia's as if the whole night had been stream-of-consciousness, a run-on sentence that lasted since they last spoke. Julia was in a similarly dreamy state and offered a brief tour like a stoned docent—"Umm books, cool stuff, Franklin has lived here for a while." The pair moved swiftly through the house into the kitchen where Julia poured them both iced coffee. Evil did not need more coffee but did not want to refuse. Julia eyed Evil, found her more dashing than usual, and thought it best to get them both outside into sensible, bright, well-behaved daylight. She led Evil across the backyard and sat down under the oak tree.

"I am sorry that I took a tone with you. I wanted to apologize."

"Okay."

"There is something I need to explain to you about my life, as of late. I am still trying to figure it out, but I don't want you to think that you hired someone who doesn't take you or your work seriously. I really do. You have no idea how much I do." Julia took a beat because she did not want to cry.

"I appreciate that."

Julia nodded. She looked at Evil and blushed.

"I'm really embarrassed, and I don't usually process things with anyone, like ever, at all, so like, I do not have a lot of practice. I haven't shared any of what I am about to say in a direct way with anyone. Not another person. I have talked to this oak tree a lot. I'm really surprised that the oak hasn't chimed in yet but maybe this is new terrain for us all."

Evil furrowed her brow, lost. She wondered if she was dreaming or still tripping, if the conversation was even real. The oak tree felt pride being included in the conversation rather than ignored like complacent scenery. The tree encouraged Julia to go for broke because there was nothing to lose.

"I don't know if I am fired, anyways." Julia shifted her body. "Whew, here goes, let me just spell it out. Ever since I moved into this house, I have been able to communicate with trees and all kinds of greenery. It started when I was late to house-sit for my brother and I killed all of his houseplants. I don't know if it was related, but the plants that were almost dead all yelled at me. And it didn't stop there. I can't control it. It's overwhelming. I went to a plant nursery and got what I can only describe as seasick. So, there was no way I could go to the woods with you. I feel like the woods would be way harder than a nursery. I hear plants sing, sometimes they heckle me, or like, this oak tree is my best friend. We process and hang out. I am okay here in this yard with this one tree. Or there is a pine tree that was pretty cool to me. Anyway, I'm doing better tuning out the hedges and the front yard, but all of it is a process. I wear headphones and play music most of the time. I realized wearing headphones all the time was not sustainable, but it is not a switch I can flip. I'm trying to learn how to manage it, but none of that is your problem. I did not realize that we would ever need to work outside of your studio. I thought being a studio assistant would mean just that. And you don't have plants at your studio, so it never came up. You probably think I am crazy now. I just wanted to tell you this in person. I understand if you need to fire me."

Evil was quiet but she looked confused. "I am getting my head around how your application to art school was based on your actual life. That it was based on how you were struggling to make sense of how this all ... suddenly happened to you."

"Yeah, it's still happening to me and I'm still trying to make sense of it. I don't want to be diagnosed or put on medication. I don't think I am having a psychotic break, you know what I mean? I am sleeping and eating and functioning in all other ways. I am totally lucid and aware. No other life forms are chatting me up. The plants are not instructing me to perform violent acts. It does not seem random. I hear very specific plants and trees, nothing else is amiss. Maybe it doesn't matter and it is some kind of disorder. I don't know yet. I'm working on it and I'm learning how to manage it myself for now. Unfortunately, I am not ready to be a decent assistant, and what I care about most just went sideways."

Julia meant her employment as a photography assistant went sideways, but Evil thought she meant her. The oak tree wanted to correct Evil but remained a quiet witness, for the moment. The tree observed the shift in Julia's energy. Evil watched Julia too; she seemed so pained and in need of help. She was gorgeous, seated on a wrinkled beach towel, dressed in a shirt with a plunging neckline and cut-off shorts. Evil lacked any coherent words, let alone full sentence construction. Her brain chemicals were still warm and floaty, gushing forth with open acceptance for all, while slowly shutting down for a reboot. Evil wanted Julia to experience her compassion and understanding. She reached for Julia and the two embraced.

"It will be okay."

Julia smiled. "Can you please tattoo those words on my arm?"

Evil's pheromones twisted Julia into a slipknot. She slid against Evil's body, kissed her neck and chewed on her ear. Evil did not anticipate the turn of events and had only meant to offer Julia a kind hug. She was supposed to hold firm boundaries. Instead, she held Julia's shirt in her hands as she licked every inch of her chest. She then discovered that Julia was not wearing underwear and all her lines in the sand washed away with the tide.

Julia finished and lay curled against Evil, who had settled her body against the oak tree. Julia stopped Evil's hands from leaving her body and pressed her fingers back between her legs. In that moment it felt like Evil's hands were the only things that kept her tethered to the earth. It was also the first time Julia did anything toppy, and she lost the plot. Evil was tired, run-through, serotonin-depleted, and not even remotely present. Her memory stirred to the night Catherine said she heard the houseplants. She began to shut down for the first time since the molly. They sat in silence. The oak tree found it all very curious. Julia suddenly felt too clingy and retreated. Evil got her hands back. She asked Julia if she smoked herbal cigarettes.

"No. That's random."

Evil nodded. She held Julia tight in her arms and then began to release her for good. It helped to not look at her face as she spoke softly into her ear, "I should go. Also, we should not do this anymore, not because you aren't a dream. Only because I am partnered. Today, what we just did, went beyond the scope of my agreement. It is all on me, I am the one who messed up and it is not your fault in any way. This is not your mess. You are great. I need to pull it together."

Julia became clear in that moment that she was over it. She did not want to be the fulcrum in another couple's relationship drama.

She thought it was above board and had signed who knows what to avoid exactly this scenario. Julia turned to face Evil. No longer the hot dagger of her dreams, she saw someone who was a little bit of a mess and knew that it was probably for the best.

"Got it. I don't want to be a problem for your relationship. I can be totally professional. We just got carried away and it won't happen again." Julia sounded remote and cold.

Julia's distance and ease caused an opposite response in Evil, who had anticipated at least some resistance. Evil's ego collapsed. She needed to be with Julia one last time to remind her how hard this should be. She grabbed her by the neck for a more aggressive farewell. Julia was confused about her own boundaries and integrity, but Evil had the spirit.

"You're Evil," Julia moaned.

When they were done, Evil repeated that it was all going to be okay, despite not knowing if that was true. Evil did not want Julia to feel rejected. After Julia's disclosure about the plants and Evil's inability to keep her hands to herself, ending their time in the backyard with a bang seemed like the best thing to do. Evil might have to fire Julia without ever being a real mentor because she could not keep it in her pants. She needed to turn the ship around. The ship being her.

Julia pulled on her clothes and grabbed her watery coffee. It was then that she realized that Evil had never undressed. Julia was embarrassed. She did not remember if she had thrown herself at Evil after emotionally melting down. Was it pity sex? She tried to table her self-disgust for later. Evil temporarily thwarted her own self-recrimination. They were a real pair, each one unable to look at the other. Julia shifted into all-business mode despite the setting. She sat on the grass well out of arm's reach and placed her coffee between them. She fixed her hair using muscle memory alone. It was time to see if she could keep her job.

"How did that shoot go?"

"The performance was wild. They made me wear a ridiculous costume."

"You wore a costume! I can't wait to see the pictures!"

"You will. I can teach you how to digitize and batch process. Then onto color correction."

"Ooh la la! Amazing. Thank you for coming over and for, like, not putting me on a psychiatric hold or whatever."

It would never have occurred to Evil to do anything like that, but Julia did not know. It had felt like a risk she needed to take if there was any hope of her continuing to be in Evil's world. Julia needed Evil to leave so she could take a bath and a long nap. She had not slept or eaten much for a time, despite her claims to the contrary. She chalked it up to the stress of missing a gig. She had never understood the whole work ethic thing until she actually wanted to *assist on the shoot and* remain employed. It was unprecedented. She was so lost in thought that she did not realize that Evil was talking to her.

"I met some really wild artists from the bay. You would have liked them. They probably talk to plants too. Maybe everyone can hear plants but me." Evil sounded flustered. What remained of her after-glow had all fizzled into a bleak arrangement. Julia was confused.

"I'm sorry. I don't know what I am saying. The shoot took a lot out of me. I don't think the coffee can keep me upright anymore. I need to go home and crash out."

Julia was unsure if her sudden professional pivot had tanked the vibe and sent Evil running. Julia wanted her to leave, but not like that. She liked it better when there was a little heat between them, but Evil was vacant. She seemed checked out, on autopilot, so Julia walked her around the side of the house to the quickest exit route. They parted with a handshake turned squeeze initiated by Julia, who had ante-upped the weirdness, then raised it to awkward. The hedges stirred the pot out of sheer boredom, "What did you to do her?"

Once home, Evil closed the shades and slept hard. She stirred in the late afternoon and was full of dread. The joyous pendulum swung back like a wrecking ball. Evil had regressed to her retired old ways. Behaviors she confronted in therapy long ago. She had need-lessly cheated on yet another partner and slipped back to using and fucked her sobriety too. What a fucker. Despite her talent for maximum chaos, it was not yet fully out of hand. She had done work on herself and had built a mountain of sobriety. She was back at base camp, blanketed in shame, but she did not drink, yet. Evil needed to go to a meeting and get her shit together. If she wanted to explore her limits, it had to be done with real integrity. She was not about to repeat old patterns and make the same mistakes that had plagued her life. She was ready for new mistakes.

* * *

Avery pulled into the driveway after Evil left for an AA meeting in his car. Neither one was aware that they had missed the other by less than five minutes. Avery opened the garage and was relieved to find a dark house. He undressed and put everything in the wash. He was more than ready to be rid of the stench of dried urine and sweat. The camping gear was easy to stow, the garage how he left it. Evil's car smelled like him, which was very bad. He left the windows down but was too tired to devise any other solutions. He showered and collapsed in the guest room. Before drifting off he realized he might scare Evil or Catherine with his presence. He had forgotten to call or text that he was returning to their home. He forced himself to post a note on the kitchen fridge to say he was there. He added a postscript to say he was asleep in the guest room.

Dreams hit hard and fast, as if they had gathered on the pillow awaiting Avery's return. He absorbed vibrations that formed words against the entirety of his body. It was hard to grasp at first, but he got the hang of it. A new language transmitted and translated. The words were basic and amounted to something like *yes, no, coming, going*. He practiced absorbing and bouncing the phrases. Coming and going were harder to form, it felt too remedial when there was so much to say. G, g, g, go, ing. Going. It got more dreamlike. He understood more about the world and his place in it as an antenna; antennas are conduits, he was a conduit, it cut both ways, flowed in both directions, a pulley system, magnets. Avery felt himself in relation to the orbs, that part was important, in relation. *Yes, no, coming, going.* The orbs appeared, making triangle shapes. He was excited and remembered his preference for that shape. One part of the triangle had to do with the antenna. He tuned into another angle and got that receivers receive. He noticed wet grass beneath his feet, he was in Evil's front yard, the orbs just overhead in a triangle shape. A cat raced up the walkway and yelled at him. Avery woke up in a cold sweat. His shirt was drenched and so were the sheets. He ran to grab a notebook and pen to write down what he could recall. He made a sketch of himself with little dashes to represent vibrations to and from an orb triangle in the sky, grass underfoot, cat in the yard. He showered, put his laundry in the dryer and remembered more from the dream. He sped back into the room, towel around his waist, and scribbled the words: yes, no, coming, going.

* * *

Evil shared at the meeting. She was honest about the past few days but painted it in broad strokes. It was the first time she had done drugs in twenty years. She nearly went to a bar instead of the meeting. What Julia confided had troubled her. She shared that her lover and her girlfriend respectively were both hearing things like houseplants talking to them, trees and such, and her son was having his own communication with UFOs. Fifth kind. She remembered that part. She was disappointed and knew her sobriety was important. Important was the understatement of two decades. Sobriety was critical to her ability to function. She mumbled something about how maybe she was a sex and love addict. Then she said, "Thank you."

Patricia wore her green work vest because she'd spilled coffee on her blouse earlier in the day. She nodded and stared intently. Evil knew Patricia was going to approach her after the meeting but then forgot about it. Patricia waited until they were in the dark parking lot to approach so it came as a surprise. Patricia's words hit Evil in the back of the neck like spitballs, "It's connected. What's happening around you." Patricia stopped dead, waiting for a reaction.

Evil was exhausted. At some point she had texted Catherine login credentials to the art program portal to view Julia's application. She asked Catherine to take a look. She wanted her to read about Julia's health issue and why she could not go to the woods. She said that Julia's essays and portfolio work were not only an art project but something very real. It was a wordy text that felt outlandishly demanding the more time that passed. Catherine did not respond for several hours and then texted that she was at the airport heading home. Evil was ashamed and felt worse after learning that Catherine had cut her work trip short. It was out of hand. Major fail.

Evil took a beat to decide if she should turn around and deal with Patricia. It was a distraction that might prove worthwhile if it quelled her urge to go see Julia. She regretted her coldness, the way she shut things down with a slam. The walls she erected were given to her, she was not their architect, and Evil had simply installed them on Catherine's behalf. It seemed like the only choice was to end things and not discuss it. She had broken their agreement, not even counting the other things she had been up to, which were at such a galactic remove that they did not seem real. Evil had to kill things with Julia because she was a grown ass adult who made an agreement with another grown ass adult. Catherine was an intelligent woman with an adventurous sexual past. She was reasonable, understanding, and there was always room for negotiation. They were not squares. Evil did not need to blast a cold hose on everything. She just needed to wait to see Julia until after she had spoken to Catherine. She was too harsh. Not cool at all. Evil was embarrassed. Julia had been so vulnerable and open. Gorgeous and soft. She did not need to do any of that.

"Hello? Where did you go? You sure you aren't receiving messages too?" Patricia smirked. She was emboldened by Evil's share and high on her clandestine knowledge.

Evil folded her arms. It was not cute or funny.

"Connected how? UFOs and plants are connected somehow?"

Patricia threw up her hands, appalled, "Shhhh! Not here, newbie!"

Evil regretted it but uttered, "Do you want to talk in my car?"

"Sunspots. It's safe there, and I'm hungry."

* * *

Sunspots Diner was the same as it ever was, and Patricia got her usual vanilla malted shake and French toast. They both had coffee.

Evil did not eat despite Patricia telling her that the food was very good there. Excellent even. Evil just wanted to get on with it.

"Okay, so how are they connected?"

"You got somewhere to be? Not here for my company, I get it. So anyway. You should know that I used to work in Intelligence. I used to work for a government outfit and had high level security clearance. Very high level. The stuff I can tell you about was declassified but not widely circulated. The other stuff I know is because I know it from first-hand experience. UFOs never abducted humans in a physical way. It was always through telepathy. Some of their methods were telepathic holds, which probably felt like abductions. People also fear homosexuality in themselves and others, and those latent fears manifest as experiences with anal probes and breeding programs. That is not what is going on here. I am not suggesting that you have a fear of anal probes or homosexuality; to the contrary, you probably enjoy them too much. You really should order something. I have to use the restroom, brb."

Evil had chosen to be here. She tabled her response and remained passively curious. It was like sitting through a questionable television show. Evil checked her phone. Catherine texted that she landed and was on her way home. Evil did the math from the time it was sent and figured she was already there. She was in their home. Evil was excited to see her, but also scared. She was uncertain what to share and what to withhold. All of it seemed unfair.

Patricia returned. She had fixed her hair into a messy bun and put on lipstick. Evil noticed blotted water on the blouse under the work vest. Many more buttons were open on the blouse. Evil needed to stay on track.

"So, there is a connection between what is happening with my partner and my son?"

"As well as the secret third thing. I left that horrible work behind years ago. Maybe they know what the third thing this is by now. Extra Terrestrials have technology that would improve all our lives. It would shift the power structures in place and have a profoundly beneficial impact for most of the population. The wealthiest people do not want things to fundamentally change, they like the power structures in place and so they fund the politicians, put people in the most important places to shoot down so-called weather balloons. There was no way for ETs to just pop down, harder with all the satellites, and so they use telepathy. And when humans go on talk shows and write books to pervert the meaning behind contact, intelligent life finds another way. A small portion of the population contains vibratory patterns and sensitivities that resonate with the ones in plant life. Psychedelic medicine has enhanced the open channels that the orbs can use to amp up the auric fields of plants. It's a backchannel. They contact us remotely because there are too many satellites and war machines preventing an actual arrival."

Evil took it in and decided to roll with the information until it snagged.

"But why would they risk showing themselves to my son, and allow him to record a video of their location, if it puts them in danger?"

Patricia adjusted her posture and tugged on the edges of her shirt to share more cleavage. She made eye-contact and seemed to address both the UFO/people conundrum as well as the Patricia/Evil one.

"It is good if everyday people are aware of their presence, so they let themselves be seen in that way for that purpose."

Evil nodded.

"I know this can be a lot to take in at once. It's stressful to comprehend the magnitude. Upsetting to know that we could all live in paradise but those in power are not going it let it happen. We could be an openly-intergalactic, thriving, healthy planet with some serious travel opportunities. So much to take in. Hard to process. I see that. I want to help. There is a stall in the restroom that has a chair in it."

Evil stood up, tossed a twenty on the table and said, "Cool, lots to think about."

"You do that."

* * *

Catherine read Avery's note on the refrigerator and laughed at the timing. She was a bit out of her mind from lack of sleep and felt unnaturally disarmed. Order would help her mental state. She took a hot shower, organized her luggage, returned clean clothing to drawers and closets. She closed her dirty laundry back into the suitcase and set it against the wall by the door. It could wait. She moisturized and pulled her hair up. Catherine layered athleisure wear over her fresh glowing skin and padded her way to the kitchen. She prepared nettle tea and rooted around for snacks. She mindlessly picked up Evil's tablet as she waited for the water to boil. She returned to an essay in *The New Yorker* that she had nearly finished on the plane and read the last few paragraphs. It was about how things fall apart and it made her sad. Without any conscious effort at her own undoing, she closed the internet app and tapped on the photo album. If Evil had walked in and asked what she was doing, she would have said she was curious to see if there were any pictures from her friend's performance in the woods, or just idle curiosity, it was hard to say for sure. Evil had not walked into the kitchen in real life and there was no one to answer to. Catherine found herself looking at a picture of her partner's E-V-I-L knuckle-inked hand on a naked woman's stomach in the foreground and her other hand inside of the woman, presumably Julia. It was taken from Julia's vantage. It was her photograph and objectively well-composed, captivating, stunning even. Catherine swiped and it was the last photo in the album. It seemed to be the only one. Catherine's thoughts jumped to the Monkey Selfie lawsuit between a nature photographer and PETA. The relationship between disparate events had to do with the photo, snapped by Julia on Evil's device, as well as the macaque's toothy grin, not that she could see Julia's face. It wasn't hard to imagine her delight. Catherine studied the image. The tablet went to sleep from lack of activity and Catherine tapped the image back to life to view it anew. She was transfixed. She even failed to hear Avery come up behind her to steal a glance over her shoulder at whatever she found so mesmerizing.

Avery averted his eyes, fell backwards, and yelped when he slammed into the cabinets.

Catherine slid the tablet away from her and across the counter.

"I'm so sorry. That was messed up. My bad. I did that."

"Let's forget about it. Sit with me for a minute?"

Avery nodded and took a seat at the kitchen table. He tried to erase the image of his mother and a woman, who he assumed to be Catherine.

"Do you want tea?"

"Thanks."

Catherine returned with a pot and two mugs.

She slipped into the chair across from him.

"I'm guessing from your note that you haven't seen her?"

"No. I got home a few hours ago then crashed."

"How are you?"

"Do you really want me to answer that? It's a lot. I don't know if I have it in me to make small talk right now, but I can try."

Catherine held her mug and considered her options.

"I am severely under slept and a bit out of my mind. I don't require small talk. Tell me, what is really going on with you?"

Avery was quiet and second-guessed his offer. "I don't know if I am breaking her trust. She told me not to tell you about the orbs, but that was so long ago, so I don't know if it was just about that one time. It got so much bigger than either of us imagined. I don't see how it is not going to come up. How could it not? She will tell you. Has she told you anything?"

"Not about that. Orbs are something I would remember."

"You are looking at me the way she did when I mentioned ETs. Let me start with a video first to save time. I will get to why we need to look it up on *AlienGuy666*'s feed later. Do you have your phone, or do we need to use *that*," Avery self-consciously pointed at Evil's tablet like it was a porno magazine. Catherine reached to the counter and forked it over. He found the video and then handed the tablet to Catherine. Her eyes widened. She recognized her neighborhood and she had to admit there were actual UFOs in the sky. It was Avery's recording, he was in it, and so she had to accept that the video was somehow real despite her cynicism. She welled up when Avery cried in the video, but assumed her reaction was overwhelm plus exhaustion. She was fascinated that it happened at the round-about above the broken plinth. UFOs or UAPs, unexplainable and phenomenal.

Avery had not intended to but told Catherine everything he remembered. The arrival of Jay, Sam, and X. His memories and fear. As he spoke it became clear that his paranoia about being surveilled was paved over with personal rage. He was uncertain about his dream, so he gave it little mention. But he was clear that an agency that left him unconscious in a random parking lot as part of a job offer was not going to ruin the best thing in his life, let alone hurt the orbs. Avery talked about his connection, the telepathic ties, and the way he could feel them arrive like a turn in the weather.

Avery's descriptions reminded Catherine of the artist Keith Haring's UFO sketches. She told Avery that Haring had said at some point that all of his figures, the thick black outlines of people, pyramids, dogs, hearts and such, were rooted in the earliest drawings he did of UFOs zapping people and dogs. Catherine searched for Haring's sketches on the tablet and showed them to Avery. Most of the lithographs were from 1982. Right there in black and white, the person was an antenna receiving energy squiggles from the ship. Avery asked her if Keith ever mentioned having direct contact, but she did not believe so. But Haring credited those drawings for birthing his oeuvre, which to Catherine's mind was not dissimilar from telepathic signals making an impression. Avery flashed to his dream, his notebook, and raced to his room, "I need to show you something."

Catherine had forgotten to drink her now tepid tea. She refilled the kettle and turned it on. She drifted far from her own problems and headlong into Avery's complicated landscape. He returned with his notebook and held up a sketch reminiscent of Keith Haring's. Clearly he was no Keith Haring or any kind of artist. But the kinship between the sketches was undeniable—perhaps it was culled from Avery's subconscious because it was an iconic image. The major departures in Avery's rendering traded out the floating hat UFO for a triangle of orbs, and in place of dogs was a cat. The electric kettle clicked off.

Avery was concerned that the agents planned to replicate his presence to attract the orbs. He did not know what would follow but did not want to be the bait. He did not know anything for sure and could not predict if the roundabout mattered. Avery stressed that the part about replicating his vibrational signature came from a memory that may or may not have been based on actual events. He needed to walk Catherine back, because he had gotten her wound up about Artificial Intelligence and Intellectual Property—Auric Property, in this case. He switched gears and said his concerns were more heightened by Sam's LED lights and Xander's sound project. Those were in the works prior to whatever happened in the desert. It was also important to note that they deleted the original videos, photos, and social media following. It was clear that the agency did not want him making videos of the orbs at the roundabout, so it seemed like that was what he should focus on doing.

Catherine liked the idea of pushing back on the agency, and as a curator her eyes were set on the roundabout as a specific site. Avery's description of the LED project sounded like stale desert art even if constructed via complex engineering. The sound project seemed equally unworthy of space on the roundabout that had been reclaimed by the will of the people. Catherine wanted the agents gone. They needed a plan akin to an intervention. Or to stage an actual intervention at the roundabout. Catherine had history at that site. She had personally helped local teens rid their neighborhood of a monument to an enslaver.

At the time, Catherine and Evil felt like they were the oldest people marching in the local George Floyd protests for Black Lives. A breakout group landed them at the Junípero Serra statue. Angsty teens defaced the statue and attempted to push it over. It was not going to yield without better tools for the job. Catherine called a fabricator friend to come lend his tools to support the teens in their spontaneous demolition. With a bullhorn Catherine informed the protestors of his arrival, who then chanted, "white truck for Black and Indigenous lives, statue removal service coming through, beep beep toot toot." They surrounded the truck bed. Her friend handed them a length of rope and latched the other side to his bumper. They cleared the plinth area for an initial beheading and then handed out sledgehammers. Neighbors watched from their windows like it was a television show or the news. Protests during a pandemic facilitated the neighborhood's disinterest in calling police or getting involved in something that seemed inevitable. It was unclear if anyone ever informed the city. Since then, the broken plinth and roundabout served as public artwork in its own right.

As Catherine recounted the story of the prior roundabout intervention, Avery lit up. "I suspected my mother was involved. But imagine my luck, I'm sitting across from the person with the skills and relationships to gum up the works of whatever martial plans are afoot. I much prefer to be in cahoots with you. You can get it done."

Catherine thrived on recognition. A certain artist who might prove useful sprang to her mind.

"So, we are in cahoots? How would you feel about giving up your room and camping in the backyard again? I have a New York-based artist that might want to help. It would probably be best to limit any communications once we get started, so they should stay here."

"Yes. That makes sense, especially after what has happened so far. Sleeping outside is better for my communication with the orbs too. I feel like we've got this. So do you want to tell me what has been going on with you?"

"Cahoots. That is what is going on with me. I have to make some calls so we can get this done."

19

Catherine met Mistake at a party in New York. Mistake was a hot potato who had been caught and released by femmes across the art world. They had swagger, confidence, and the talent to back it up. Catherine was attracted to the twenty-six-year-old sculptor but kept it professional for all the reasons. Mistake noticed when Catherine avoided houseplants at a party and positioned herself close to the music speakers. They had listened to a podcast on the way to the party, a story about telepathic tendencies and failed attempts to tune them out. Mistake inquired about Catherine's spatial decisions with a twinkle in their eye. She was coy at first, but Mistake disarmed her with a moving conversation. It was an elegant dance, Mistake waxed on about the struggles of the painter Agnes Martin but had simultaneously spoken to Catherine's own mental landscape. It hit close to home in a soft and generative fashion. Mistake pierced a veil without knowing any details. Closeted about her talking-plant situation, Catherine had not thought of it in that way prior to their chat. Catherine's inner voice agreed with Mistake, she would end up alone in a lifeless desert if she continued to outrun her own new reality, overbooking it or strategically working a room in order to avoid houseplants. The eye candy before her was all the more reason to remain at large in the world, an active member of society. Mistake was a revelation who flirted and held eye-contact beyond reason. Their name was also a helpful reminder not to cross a very sexy line at the end of the night, and a few hours later when they texted. She had taken the minor risk of giving them her phone number. Catherine did not share her personal contact information often, but something made her want a direct line to Mistake rather than communicating through her gallery.

Catherine felt a bit nervous scrolling to their contact, but given the stakes, it was worth it. The roundabout project was well within their wheelhouse and the site already had a vacant plinth. She needed to act immediately to catch Mistake, and also to put in a call to her friend at the Whitney Independent Studio Program before Evil returned home. Catherine took a selfie in front of the bathroom pin-up lady decoupage to grab Mistake's attention. It worked. They were visiting a friend's mushroom farm in Oregon and more than ready for another adventure. Catherine used her miles to book them a ticket.

* * *

The following day, Evil retrieved Mistake from the airport, overwhelmed from the moment they appeared. Evil juggled conflicting desires to be them, fuck them, and also, to put them back on a plane in the opposite direction. Facial tattoos and half sleeves, a delicate mustache, sinewy body with muscular arms, plus they smelled like an outdoor gym in a burnt forest. Evil worried her animated response to their presence prompted Mistake to put on a hoodie and sunglasses.

"Can I smoke? They're herbal."

Evil nodded. Mistake smoked herbal cigarettes just like Catherine. Evil did not know if it was a flex or a coincidence. Evil was a visual learner. Catherine had made her point. The lesson that unfolded as Evil drove home had elucidated why Catherine did not want to process the night before. Why do all that emotional labor when you can simply fly in the sword of Damocles? Evil was afraid of Catherine's endgame. Evil did not want to lose her love to some stupidly hot twenty-six-year-old artist. Evil saw what she did there. It stabbed her in the heart in a formidably beautiful way, and Evil bled out from behind the wheel—metaphorically speaking. Mistake chain smoked herbal cigarettes which seemed absurd enough for Evil to judge them.

"This is it. Go on in. Catherine is expecting you. I have a meeting."

"Thanks, friend."

Mistake jumped from the car with their two black bags. Evil watched using only her peripheral vision. She drove away unsure what would happen next. She had the thought that her self-portrait above the bed would put the kibosh on using the bedroom for sex with someone other than her. Evil's heart sank when she remembered that she had sullied the bedroom with Julia. She was a terrible person and cheered for Catherine in the way one might root for a cinematic villain who was more appealing than the protagonist. Maybe Evil could watch them? That seemed like an evolved way to stay engaged with her partner as they took the sharp corner.

She pulled over and typed that question as a text message to Catherine but did not hit send. Catherine's intentions were never made clear, and it might be seen as hostile to assume that she was going to have sex with Mistake. The only way Evil would survive Mistake's visit was if she could return to her studio and find a way to prove to Catherine that the mess she made had artistic value. It was only part of her process. Evil had not yet revisited anything she had shot with Julia or from the motel. She prayed that her madness had meaning and that it bore fruit. It seemed like her best move was to find the goods, stack her hand, and dazzle her partner with her accomplishments. Evil pulled back into traffic right as a text message arrived from Catherine. She had decided to host a dinner party. She told Evil to invite Julia.

* * *

Avery and Mistake were on the sidewalk within sight of the roundabout. Mistake instructed Avery to take measurements of the plinth while they hung back. Avery crossed the street, uncertain if any agents had eyes on him. He did not clock any vans or mysterious vehicles. "Get in, get out, kid," he whispered aloud, like a coach or the dad he never had. Avery worked quickly. His heart raced like he was about to get caught shoplifting. He wanted to calm down and appear nonchalant. It was embarrassing to have his anxious constitution, given that he was a straight cis white man in America. What did he really need to worry about aside from some random military agency? He needed to work on himself and get therapy. Avery finished measuring. He shoved the paper and pen in his pocket and clipped the metal tape case onto his waistband.

He returned on the opposite side of the street from Mistake. He improvised. He wondered what someone like Mistake, who was underground-famous for defacing property and installing unsanctioned public art, thought about his nerves of tin. He hoped Mistake did not regret their involvement in the ridiculous-seeming but actually very important situation. To flush the anxiety from his system, Avery replayed his dream from the night before. In the dream, he was in a tent in the backyard, Sam's fist was lodged in his mouth as she gave him a blowjob. His recollection was too vivid. He overshot and got aroused. He willed his mind towards something bad and jumped to the Joshua Tree parking lot. A real boner killer. The agents pretended to be his peers and left him unconscious in a parking lot.

* * *

Julia rejected all of her clothes. She had no clue what to wear to dinner. She wanted to look non-threatening but still hot and stylish, a particular vibe that her wardrobe lacked. Julia was terrified, but in a healthy-fear kind of way. Evil shared the invite with the caveat that it was "Late Notice," so she understood if Julia was "Unavailable." Evil capitalized the words "Late Notice" and "Unavailable," but Julia played stupid. There was no way Julia would miss it. She wanted to witness firsthand whatever chaos was about to unfold. Julia decided that she should never turn down an invitation from Catherine, not in this lifetime. Especially after she read a message on Evil's studio social media account that implied that she was up to no good in more ways than just Julia. It had reassured her that Evil had made a far bigger mess of her relationship than whatever boundary they had transgressed. Julia had been part of a series of bad decisions and, for whatever reason, that stung less. Julia needed Catherine to like her and wanted to continue to work for Evil, even if it meant killing her feelings. It was the first time she ever felt goal oriented. She needed an outfit to reflect her new inner clarity. She was determined to make friends.

She found a black jumpsuit in Franklin's closet that fit her well. It zipped all the way down the front to well between her legs, a marvelous detail (especially for the bathroom and whatever other mischief Franklin got up to). Julia put on hoop earrings. After final hair adjustments in the bathroom mirror, she added a bold lip. She raided the kitchen cabinets and found an unopened box of fancy dark chocolate pretzels to give the false impression that she was the kind of adult person that never showed up empty-handed to a dinner party. Then came a major decision, to smoke weed or not to smoke weed, or split the difference?

* * *

Dance music spilled from Julia's headphones. She was forcing a mood. Her door knock was met by the hand of a laughably hot person in the threshold. Her pulse quickened. Mistake squeezed then lowered her hand while looking into her eyes. They shut the door and escorted Julia to the front porch instead of going inside. They pulled an herbal cigarette from a witchy tin and offered one to Julia. It was all incredibly presumptuous, but how could she refuse? Julia lowered her headphones around her neck and let the beats continue as ambiance. Names were exchanged and cigarettes smoked. They both faced away from the house and towards the empty street. Mistake bumped against Julia, shoulder to shoulder, and then shared a side-long gaze. When neither looked away, it turned into a staring contest that lasted until Julia's eyes started to burn. Mistake clasped Julia's zipper-pull and declared, "I won. I want a prize." Julia reached into her tote and handed them the pretzels.

Julia followed Mistake down the hall. She felt more relaxed until they entered the kitchen. Catherine introduced herself, air-kissed Julia's cheeks, and squeezed her arm. She was stunningly gorgeous and smelled expensive, like a leather purse stuffed with figs set upon a sand dune. Julia wanted to bend a knee and pledge her house loyalty.

Catherine winked at her. Julia felt an intense gaze and she and Avery locked eyes. Catherine introduced her to Avery as Evil's assistant. She shot out her hand quickly and said, "Hi, I'm Julia."

Avery smirked, "You're very familiar. Do we know each other? I think we must." He looked under slept. Julia had to tread lightly since Avery seemed loopy. She claimed to just have "one of those faces." Mistake cut in with a wry compliment, "Hardly," then handed Julia a glass of hibiscus lemonade. They lingered beside her. Catherine cleared her throat. "I guess you two have met." Julia felt like a horny slut already. She moved her body away from the others to the safety of the asexual chips and guacamole on the counter. The table was set for five, a horribly unstable number linked with the most annoying tarot cards, games and defeat. She was doomed. Julia had never been in the kitchen or dining area before. It was helpful to be in a common space distant from any bedrooms. Mother and son, like a terrible porn. Thankfully, the son had done little more than touch her boob. Unmemorable at best, and hopefully Avery would forget it ever happened; she certainly had until now. Last she'd heard, he'd swapped cars with Evil and left town on a camping trip. Unfortunately, he'd made it back.

"Hey!" Evil rushed in with foil trays and brown bags from a plant-based Mexican restaurant. Mistake helped place the spread on the butcher block. Evil gave Julia a butch nod, which Catherine found hilarious. Julia disassociated into her beverage and imagined that she was safely seated on an ice cube in the pink water. Avery had spent enough time around queer sexual tension to read a room. He assumed everyone was hot for Mistake—hell, even he was—and never considered the far more complex constellation at play.

"So, Julia, how did you end up working for my mom?" Avery asked to reset the vibes. He was honestly curious and a little creeped out. Before Julia decided how to respond, Evil jumped in. She spoke quickly, as if she might speed up the evening and send everyone on their way, "Julia applied for the art program, and I liked her portfolio. Catherine encouraged me to get an assistant. And voilá. Shall we sit or bring plates over here?" The pace felt intense. All eyes went to Catherine who distilled languid aplomb, "The three of you decide. I need to speak to Julia in private for a moment." Julia was mortified but resisted looking to Evil for help. Evil had none to offer. She was equally nervous and busy hiding it, plus she'd given Julia an out she failed to take.

Julia trailed Catherine's perfectly painted silver toenails. The vibrant living room had several large gold baroque mirrors and works of art that made Julia swoon, "What is your life?" Catherine appreciated Julia's ease.

Catherine sat on the couch and patted for Julia to sit down right beside her. She pulled out her phone and moved even closer to Julia once she sat down, and then tucked one leg beneath her body. On the phone screen was the image of Evil's hand on Julia's stomach and her other hand between her legs. Catherine showed it to Julia so they could look at it together. Julia had never seen the image aside from the moment she had taken it. Her stomach caved in on itself and a pond of sweat formed under her armpits. She had no idea what one says in this type of situation. It was awful. Maybe Catherine knew everything.

Catherine was unreserved, "At first, I wanted to crumple you up like a sheet of paper then throw you into the trash. But this is powerful, objectively so." Catherine swiped to the next image, Julia's photo of the hedge with an orange leaf blower in the background. She swiped a few more times and it was clear that she had pulled a few select photos and Polaroids from Julia's portfolio.

Julia did not understand how she had the photos on her phone and wondered if that was legal. Given that her reality had become the slick underside of a banana peel, "legal" was a silly thought, more of a desperate need for a foothold. Her insecurity made her wonder if she would melt into a stain on their furniture. A stain they would call "Julia" and hide under pillows or flip the cushion to fully vanquish.

Catherine saw Julia's confusion and delighted in it a tad, while seemingly being stoic. "I hope it is alright that I shared these with a friend at the Whitney Independent Studio Program. We both agreed that you should apply. The deadline just passed, but I got you a brief extension. I can help you with your application, but we must submit it no later than this week. Here is my contact info." Catherine pulled a business card from the pocket of her phone case and handed it to Julia, who looked embarrassed.

"Do you know about that program?"

Julia shook her head, "I've heard of the Whitney Biennial, but I don't know much about how you actually get a career in the arts. My half-brother Franklin made me apply to art school. It's all new to me, aside from being a fan of art and going to see stuff. I know you're an important curator and gallerist. I feel like I should just do anything that you think that I should do."

"Well, I agree with Franklin and am glad he made you apply. I related to your work. Like you, I have been dealing with a plant situation as of late. So, I have a serious stake in the conversation. If you, Julia as an artist, create work around the experience, it offers shape to the conversation, and that holds value for everyone. Having the ability to hear plants is incredibly isolating. I overbook myself just to avoid it."

"Does that work?"

Catherine laughed. "It has proved isolating in other ways but was a useful strategy for a time. That is over now. I'm out of my shell. I doubt that we are the only two people with this thing, and I prefer to be part of a broader collective."

"Do you know why this is happening to us?"

"I wanted to talk with you about the program in private because I did not want to put you on the spot. It would mean moving to New York. I suppose you will need to think about that. I did not mention it to Evil. It's entirely your decision. I think you have an excellent shot at being accepted. As far as the big *why*, I don't know, but that conversation is one we can have over dinner. Let's go eat jackfruit tacos and talk about aliens. I'm famished."

Julia wanted to refuse and insist the pair stay put. Julia finally had a chance to talk about plant-telepathy with someone who understood exactly what she had been going through. She lingered on the couch trying to work up the nerve to ask Catherine to wait. Her courage was adrift. She rushed to follow Catherine's swift gait. Puzzled by the mention of aliens, Julia quickly remembered Avery's stupid orbs. As far as she could sense, it was unlikely that he would share that she was the one he brought home that night, but time would tell. Julia was troubled by Catherine's access to her application materials. She wondered if Evil shared them with her to help decide to make her an assistant or not. But that did not account for the more recent sex photo. None of it really mattered, but something was curious. What was Catherine's game?

Julia followed Catherine's lead and filled up her plate with colorful tacos at the butcher block. Catherine took her seat next to Evil and left the remaining one next to Mistake. Julia felt the electricity return as she sat down beside them. The dinner conversation revealed that Mistake lived in New York. Julia tried to soften her involuntary smile at the prospect of a future in a shared city and then felt like a dog betrayed by the tell of its own tail. She suddenly understood that Catherine had noticed her smile by the domino experience of her own similar tell. Her joyful reaction had been orchestrated. She suspected that she was being redirected away from Evil in a sly career-and-lust-boosting fashion, a push so subtle it was like the invisible hand of fate. Julia's water went down the wrong pipe and she coughed. If she stopped breathing, surely, Catherine would resuscitate her, for Catherine was a femme goddess, if a sneaky one. Bend the knee, Julia! Make a sacrifice to Catherine's altar. At the very least stop coughing at Catherine's dinner table, despite the thrill of Mistake's hand on her back, all of their eyes searching to make sure she was okay.

Avery noticed an intergenerational twinning across the table but did not know how to raise his observation without sounding homophobic, ageist, or out of his lane. It was an artistic rendering of sorts, Evil and Catherine opposite Julia and Mistake. Unmistakable from Avery's vantage, like a modern spin on a classic. Avery held his thoughts but relished an opportunity to ask Julia personal questions that she never would have tolerated from him. "So, Julia, are you from here?"

Julia finished a bite of her taco and took a minute to be annoyed that Avery started his questions for her with "So." She shook her head. After she swallowed the delicious vinegar-laced bite, she offered the table some insight. "My half-brother lives nearby. I'm house-sitting while he's away on the Rome Prize. He's writing his third novel." Julia was unsure why she felt so open taking pride in Franklin's success. It was gross and unlike her. It was probably because Catherine had rattled her insides then buttered them up. She felt squishy and ready to embrace whatever Catherine doled out. If she was being killed with kindness she would die happily, swaddled by handsome arty queers. Avery dug in, "Are your parents out here as well or where are they?"

"My parents are dead." Coldness returned to her eyes. Ahh, Julia was back. Her agency returned with a thud.

Mistake leaned towards Julia, "My parents are dicks."

"Mine are dead," Catherine said flatly, and Evil went in for the win, "Mine, are dead dicks, salute!" She raised a glass, they all toasted. As they touched glasses, Julia and Evil held brief eye-contact for the first time that night. It hurt her heart, but Julia held down her new role as a pleasant, professional studio assistant.

Avery refused the toast and ate the rest of his meal in silence.

Evil spent the entire meal fixated on whatever had transpired between Catherine and Julia in their private aside. Had Catherine mentioned her brief relapse or asked any questions about their sex life? It was hard to imagine either, but the two of them alone was far afield. Evil tired of Mistake's presence and whatever threat they posed. The moment Mistake excused themself to use the restroom, Evil chose to move things along. She stood up to clear the table and dropped her only bomb, "I heard that the orbs have technologies that would benefit humanity and the planet, but those in power want to remain in power. They do not want a better world. They want this one. If you were an ET flying around with all that knowledge to share but unable to land, the best way to transmit it would be remotely. So, how do you get that information to people? Telepathy." Catherine was surprised that Evil had any thoughts on the matter.

Julia was skeptical, "If the orbs are causing us to be telepathic with plants and there is some kind of agenda, the plants don't seem to know that. Maybe it's all the fertilizer, but plants talk a lot of shit.

They've also been here the longest and are intuitive and wise and have the insight and technology to help the planet. Do plants need orbs to tell them what to do?"

Avery yes/and-ed, "If everything is about vibrations and signals and auric fields, it makes sense that the orbs caused it, or it's somehow related."

Julia crossed her arms and slumped into the dining chair. "Great, if your orbs are so invested, why don't you get them to land and fix things around here, not just hit us with vibey gossip rays or whatever?"

"It's more like consciousness-raising," Avery corrected and left the table with the remaining plates.

Julia mouthed, "Whatever."

The room was silent. Catherine put on the kettle and leaned against the counter. It was hard to avoid the feeling that she and Julia were dealing with experiences that the others could never fully comprehend.

"Evil, honey, when did you put all that together?"

Evil paused washing dishes and enjoyed holding the room's attention. Mistake was finally elsewhere. She was reluctant to give up Patricia as her source. She crossed the sink and spoke directly to Catherine. She only wanted to speak to Catherine and wished everyone else would leave.

"There's an intense character I know from meetings. We talked about telepathy, and she said there was a connection between the orbs and plants. We had a quick chat at a diner. I don't know if she is for real but none of it is weirder than anything else that has happened." Evil put her palm on Catherine's lower back and studied her face.

Julia broke in, "It's Patricia from the Plant Nursery, isn't it? Did you go to Sunspots with her?"

"It was an Anonymous person."

Mistake slipped back into the kitchen with a sketchbook and listened with great interest.

"Patricia is bananas. Did she insult you at the end, so you had to pay the check to get out of there? She does that, like, all the time. The server told me. It's her thing. She lures people to that diner and then causes a scene to get them to pay the check."

"No. She may have hit on me, but that doesn't matter."

"She told me I was a horny slut who better keep all of this to myself. She called me a photosympathizer and threatened me."

Mistake laughed inappropriately then apologized. Julia laughed because it was so stupid. Evil turned back towards the sink. She really wanted everyone gone.

Avery was frustrated by all the laughter, "There are agents that want to control the orbs and minimize orb contact. Telepathy with orbs is destabilizing on a global scale. It implies that anyone with telepathy can probably communicate directly with aliens, and they see that as a national security threat. Even cat psychics are being harassed and threatened. We know something important is happening. Even if this anonymous-Patricia person knows what she is talking about, I don't really get how that impacts us. Catherine, we should just stick to our plan."

Julia glared at Avery, and Evil was caught off-guard. "What plan?"

* * *

Avery retired to the tent in the backyard while the dinner party continued. He needed privacy to contact the orbs. He did not need to speculate. He had a direct line. Avery tried to recall the language from his dream. Coming, going, yes, and no. The vibrations were foggy. He gave Mistake all of his notes but wanted them back. He realized that he could just go inside and ask. Avery squatted at the front of the tent and saw that the kitchen lights were off. The party had ended or moved to another space. Avery shut the flap.

Mistake had asked Avery if there was anything else to consider for the sculpture. Logistics were already in place, and most of the design, but Avery felt like something was missing. It would draw Public attention to the roundabout and the orbs. Avery wanted to discuss the plan with the orbs themselves. He also did not know what to make of Julia's plant-telepathy experiences. They did not seem to amount to anything. Catherine had even less to say about any useful exchanges. It seemed like too much time had passed since he last had direct contact with the orbs, and he felt out of the loop.

In order to tune back in, Avery imagined the roundabout and pictured orbs in a triangle shape overhead. Instead, memories that resurfaced at Pyramid Lake haunted him. He was no longer able to conjure the roundabout without thinking about being restrained in Joshua Tree, the video loop of himself playing. His experience was at a remove, the video layered on top of it like plastic shrink wrap trapping his actual memory. His main connection had been fully juiced. He felt like pulp circling the sink drain of the universe, a black hole in his brain.

It might have been the sleeping bag, or the tent, or some sub-conscious response to whatever smell remained, that caused Avery's extreme discomfort. Unsettled, he wondered if he needed therapy rather than revenge. No one put much stock in recovered memories, but something had happened in Joshua Tree. He was violated and left unconscious in an abandoned parking lot. He turned on the lantern and used the burner phone's final battery life to send a text. The one notebook he did not give to Mistake held the number he needed. Avery's hand shook as he texted, Fuck You, to NDA. He hit send and the battery died. The move tapped out Avery's adrenals. He thought about his conversation with Catherine and the Keith Haring work that she had shown to him. There was an untitled ink and spray enamel piece from a 1980 show at PS 122 that depicted a UFO beaming red squiggly zaps onto a naked couple doing it doggy style. Avery thought about Sam and their shared interests. That couple could have been them sharing space zaps, but instead she was a shady Government Op. He barely even cared about her anymore. His heart and body were longing for the UFO. He was sad when he fell into a hard sleep.

* * *

Avery stirred, Sam was in his tent. Another Sam sex dream. Why was he wired this way? Her hair was back this time. Her illuminated LED watch made them both visible. Avery sat up and opened his sleeping bag. He reached over and pulled Sam towards him, drew her hand towards his sweatpants.

"What that fuck are you doing, Avery? I'm not here to fuck you, asshole. I came to warn you. Tomorrow night they plan to mimic your auric field and amplify it to draw out the orbs. You are not someone that has been forgotten. The stakes are high."

Sam crawled towards the flaps.

Avery's voice cracked, "I'm so sorry! I thought I was dreaming! I swear! I've been having dreams about you. That sounds bad too. I know. I'm sorry. Really." He folded his head into his hands.

Sam paused momentarily.

He looked up at her, "What should I do to stop them? What do you want me to do? I'll do it."

Sam shrugged and turned off her watch. The remaining light came from the open tent fabric. She was half outside when she whispered, "I don't know, but they have eyes on you. Don't poke bears with meaningless tantrums."

"You're NDA?"

"I'm a warning system."

She stepped outside.

Avery pleaded, "Sam?"

He could not make out her face when she popped her head inside, "Stop dreaming about me. Warn the orbs."

"But how? I can't connect with them anymore."

Then she was gone.

20

Asleep under a pile of folded towels, Edith dove across the frequencies until she dropped into the part of her subconscious that contained emergency protocols. She had hit the limits of possiblilty as an indoor cat and it was time for her next steps. Henry was preoccupied and no longer noticed basic safety measures to keep her inside. She slipped through the open bathroom window and leapt seven feet to the tree without incident. She jumped down from a branch no less than eight feet in the air and darted towards the park. Honestly, she was angry with Henry. She did not even look back.

Once she entered the park grounds, she hid. If the right elements were not present, she would have to linger or seek help. Given Henry's actions, time was of essence. Everything that was now required of her felt unappealing, she wanted catnip to take the edge off. She had to locate specific energy to make contact, but if she happened to catch a lizard in the meantime, all the better. The park overstimulated her and it was hard to remain linear. She was distracted for hours before finding her footing.

Edith noticed a small encampment in the distance. Before it, tall grass stood along a tiny pond; she made a run for it and crept into a nook at the base of a tree. She didn't smell anything of concern and was well out of sight. Edith needed to be certain that she would remain undisturbed. After an instinctual amount of time passed without incident, she allowed her consciousness to expand and attempted telepathic contact with the orbs.

Edith transmitted her signal. The ETs locked into her auric field. Edith was frustrated with the conversation. Yes, she had a sweet deal and one key responsibility—her mission in life, her purpose. She tried her best to keep Henry on a leash and had been successful until the surprising turn. She'd told Henry *no*. It was not her fault that his ambitions quadrupled in the face of social media. She did not understand why hyper-intelligent beings involved humans in their plans in the first place. That was on them, not her!

Edith received a brief, regionally specific history lesson focused on recent efforts in the U.S. Their telepathic outreach began with a direct line to humans, but a military spin program started in the '50s made it impossible to continue, especially given that the program's mandate was to create a horrible public image of intergalactic travelers. They encountered a paradox: despite an endless fascination with aliens from outer space, higher intelligence was unwelcome. They had to regroup, but agreed telepathy was the best entry point to establish contact because it only required overlapping energy fields to be legible on each end. There was a period of incremental communication and much failure.

Edith learned the last push to share life-enhancing technology on a massive scale transpired in the '70s and coincided with a spike in psychedelic consumption. People were more open. Then there was a legislative onslaught to kill psychedelic research and recreational use. The ETs lost their gains. Focus shifted to increasing the auric energy fields of select plants, fungi, dogs, and cats in the late '70s and early

'80s. Expansive auras boosted a wide range of contact and made for easier telepathic reading. But dogs and fungi were too loose-lipped when they were tested with clandestine messages. Felines and flora responded well to the auric enhancement and have been the focus ever since. Cats wielded additional power like natural leaders. Smugness was the main tell of their expanded abilities.

When they augmented the cats' auric fields their subsequent increase in influence was masked by their popular rise on the internet. Houseplant auras hit their peak vibration during the global pandemic years, masked by plant daddyism and gentrification. Since these accomplishments, the ETs had gone unnoticed transmitting information to cats and plants. Cats and plants were independently prepared to receive and share evolutionary insight. The first phases were successful, broader energy fields primed interspecies communication, but telepathy between cats and plants hit a major wall. It did not matter how much the auric frequencies were raised on either side, cats inevitably destroyed plants—terrible for collaborative efforts. Humans were once again the focus, for the first time since the early '80s. But things were lopsided. Psychedelics had regained popularity, restoring back-channels to life improving technologies, along with legislation to make them a mainstay. However, the conservative stranglehold on culture was on par with the '80s. There was no way conservative global power structures would allow direct communication with ETs to influence the future, even if they did want to share sustainable solutions to benefit all life on the planet.

Edith understood where she entered the story, and the current problem with telepathic visibility; the timing was off, a corrupt legislative onslaught would arise to prevent humans from engaging in telepathy despite the fact that only 0.5 percent of the population had their auric fields expanded. The powers that be did not want life for most people to improve. The cultural landscape was in a dark timeline. They would either need to shut down the entire effort at this very critical juncture or improvise a new strategic response. *Ahem.*

The history lesson concluded, and Edith crossed her paws. Henry had jumped the gun and now things were in motion way too soon. Edith was contemplative before transmitting her response. Felines and flora were at maximum auric field reach and receptivity. Humans were part of the equation and could not be eliminated. She would destroy a plant, no question about it, and had to be honest. She mostly adored Henry despite his self-centered, impetuous, defiant nature, which only reminded her of her birth family. But regardless of human limitations and the irritation of plants, Edith knew what came next. She had the ability to telepathically instigate next moves with her own kind en masse. She summoned the one great intergenerational truth passed down from her ancient ancestors and shared it as her only response, "Direct action gets the goods." She returned to the waking world without further meow.

* * *

The night wound down on the porch. Mistake ran out of herbal cigarettes, but Catherine was flush. She slipped inside and returned with the same witchy pre-roll tin as Mistake. Evil made a mental note. Evil joined in to interrupt the spell between the pair; if it meant she had to take up smoking again, so be it. Despite her best efforts, Evil hung in the doorway and sulked. Julia asked Mistake about life in New York. Mistake offered to walk her home and tell her all about it. Julia instinctively looked to Catherine and Evil for permission. Mistake noticed her deference and without missing a beat added, "And maybe we can all go by the roundabout?" Catherine agreed as Evil declined.

Their walk was crowded with wild anecdotes about New York City that left little room for chatty greenery. Julia longed for her own stories about the city and throbbed with intrigue. She definitely wanted to apply to the studio program and would ask for Catherine's help regardless of her motive. Julia led them up the porch and inside. Mistake immediately asked Julia if she had any weed and if it was okay for them to snoop around to retrieve it. Julia told Mistake where to find her stash and led Catherine to the back-yard. Julia hoped Mistake would do something incredibly perverse with her belongings but resisted saying so.

Julia used the excuse of introducing Catherine to the oak tree to get her alone. There was a tension that hung between them like foreboding clouds, despite Catherine's willingness to act like every-thing was totally cool. Rather than cutting to the chase, Julia took the longest way around. She needed the oak to help her navigate the conversation, and also, if the oak was willing, help return things to an equilibrium. Julia caressed the soft wrinkled bark at its base.

Catherine readjusted to the direction the night seemed to take. She thought she was just dropping Julia off, but Mistake seemed to have other plans. Catherine had not spent much time in the outdoors, but decided that if Julia could handle it, she better figure it out too. Julia opened up to Catherine about her break-up with Reggie. She explained she was a month late to the house-sit, and recounted how the dying houseplants had told her what a terrible person she was, how maybe they were correct. She felt like a terrible person. Catherine was quietly thankful that she was no longer in her twenties, despite missing the energy and her younger body. She decided that Julia was an attractive person. Julia sensed that Catherine was checking her out. They were both relieved when Mistake reemerged with outdoor cushions and blankets from the garage. The mood shifted, the air growing lighter as they arranged the pillows and blankets. Mistake was an egalitarian flirt. They proceeded to get everyone high then and disappeared back into the house once more to get some water.

Julia admired Catherine, and wondered what would happen if she simply spoke her mind.

"Would it help things if we slept together?"

Catherine laughed.

Julia blushed. She wanted to blame her stupidity on being high. Instead, she panicked and overshared, "So, like, you know how I run Evil's social media account for her studio, so, I saw the messages about her and those hot queers from Oakland, and you are so gorgeous and totally amazing and I thought if you were …"

Catherine's eyes narrowed. "Show me." She felt impatient as Julia slowly located Evil's studio account and scrolled to find the messages. Julia hoped they'd been deleted, and she could back pedal. The oak tree attempted to dissuade Catherine from going down Julia's rabbit hole, but it was too late. Catherine read the brief exchange, got the drug-fueled orgy vibe, and tossed Julia's phone onto the blanket by her foot.

Catherine sighed, "Hopefully her new work is worth whatever happens next. Have you seen any of it?"

Julia shook her head.

Catherine leaned against the tree and the oak asked what she needed. Catherine's thoughts turned to Mistake, and she allowed her desire to surface right as they emerged with a pitcher of water and three glasses. So thirsty. Julia felt spun out and excused herself to use the restroom. Once inside, she realized that Evil might never forgive her, and Catherine might think she hoped to damage their relationship beyond repair for her own ends. But Julia did not have ends!

Julia's primary goal was to hide for a few minutes, but once she was in the bathroom, she made use of it. She changed her hair and cleaned up her eye make-up. Julia had not looked in a mirror for hours, not since before she left the house. Sometimes she forgot that she had a face and body that other people could see. Mostly, she felt like a warm sack with a few ideas and horny impulses. Her thoughts were riddled with self-doubt, but she did possess some resolve. She had offered to sleep with Catherine to balance the scales. It was the kind of offer, whether accepted or rejected, that would have given *her* comfort if she had been in that position. She did not anticipate her generosity would fall flat and be laughed off. Her interpersonal compass was broken. Reggie had really done a number on her. When they first started to date, Reggie had said, "Everyone just goes around trading heartbreaks." Was Julia selfishly trying to heal from her last relationship by ruining someone else's partnership? She'd started the night wanting to repair things and just made everything so much worse. She needed to salvage her relationship with Catherine and get accepted into the program in New York. Then they could be free of her. Julia wished she could be free of herself too.

It was time to be a better host. Julia gathered candles and then grabbed a box of popsicles. She stood in front of the freezer for an inordinate amount of time with the popsicles in her hand. She wondered if the colorful treats were an alarming choice. Catherine was a professional adult woman. Julia threw the box back into the freezer. Candles were unimpeachable. She was too high, paranoid even. It was why she rarely smoked more than a hit or two around other people. Too late. She looked for her lighter then remembered it was outside.

Julia returned to her guests, candles in hand. Halfway into her grass-lined strut, she realized Catherine and Mistake were making out under her oak tree. She froze. She watched them kiss, unsure what to do with herself. Catherine pulled away from Mistake and waved Julia towards them. "Come here. I don't know what we are doing." Julia did as told. Mistake danced around, "I know what we are doing! Hold hands and encircle the oak!" They circled three times and then hugged the oak. All three pressed themselves against the tree. A warm syrupy feeling filled Julia's body and her consciousness uncorked. Mistake stroked and kissed Catherine and Julia's hands. Julia and Catherine exchanged a look of wonder. It was hard to know if it was the weed or the dopamine rush, but something had shifted. It was like they were in communion with the entire yard. There was no separation, as if they, too, had sprung from the earth, like the life all around them.

Mistake kissed Catherine. Catherine continued to hold Julia's hand. Julia liked the feeling of Catherine's tight, unrelenting grip, the warmth that radiated between their palms. Mistake choreographed their bodies, then announced they were ambidextrous, to which Catherine purred, "Prove it." Catherine turned towards Julia. She kissed her out of sheer curiosity and was surprised, shocked even, by their intense chemistry. Mistake did not overstate their own abilities, but in the middle of what was turning out to be a very fun and pleasurable time for all—including the oak tree—a fluffy grey cat ran across the yard. The cat stood a few feet from Mistake and yelled at them. At first Mistake made a joke and asked where it was headed in such a hurry, but they were suddenly able to carry on a full conversation. With a cat. Julia and Catherine watched on, hearing only Mistake and not the cat. The cat darted away. Mistake stood, grabbed their clothes, and ran off into the night, presumably after the cat.

Catherine was turned on, close, and frustrated by Mistake. She reached for Julia who, about to chase after Mistake, stopped to kiss her once more. Julia was immensely excited, not only from receiving a passionate kiss, but from a woman who kept her own time. It had never occurred to Julia that she did not have to scramble after someone who ran after a cat. Julia inhaled Catherine's perfume, bit her earlobe, and choked her while bringing her to orgasm.

"What made you take that picture?"

"What picture?"

"Oh, I think you know the one."

Julia poured glasses of water to stall. She felt ashamed.

"I don't think any answer would be honest. I was out of my mind. Maybe it was a tiny stab at control?"

"You should think about those things to be able to speak about your work." Catherine stretched, "Anyways, I feel better now."

"That's probably the oak tree."

"Probably."

Catherine poured water onto the ground around the oak tree then kissed its bark to say thank you. She took a sip of water and gazed at Julia, who had zipped back into her jumpsuit.

Julia found an unexpected kindness in Catherine. She wanted to reach for her, but assumed their transaction was now complete. Julia hugged the oak tree instead. Catherine went inside to freshen up and Julia trailed behind her, both of them unclear what to do about Mistake's sudden flight.

* * *

Catherine and Julia decided to check the roundabout. They quickly discovered that plant-induced seasickness abated from the small act of holding hands. It was hard to believe at first, but after a simple test of letting go and then holding hands once more, there you had it: Telepath Dramamine. Catherine was not much of a hand holder, so it was less comfortable for her than Julia, who was delighted at the prospect. She found it remarkably beautiful that holding hands with another plant-telepath was the cure. Julia felt incredibly expansive, like she was in league with the plants and trees and the entire neighborhood. Catherine held a similar sense of an interconnected world. It reminded her of her LSD days of yore. It was as if the two walked in place as the world turned beneath their feet. They pondered aloud if it was the weed, but it was so much more about their own shifted consciousness than being on drugs, maybe two plant-telepaths together amplified things as well. Plus, it was Julia's weed, and she certainly had not felt anything like this before. Mistake was not visible but Catherine spotted two suspicious vans parked nearby. One had an open door that revealed black Pelican cases piled high. It was eerie. They doubled back towards the house and hoped Mistake had done the same.

* * *

Mistake was in Avery's tent when Catherine and Julia arrived, sketching an image they received from the grey cat. It involved a number of ferns that looked like satellite dishes along the perimeter of the roundabout. Mistake folded the drawing and handed it to Catherine as they stepped back out onto the grass. She mentioned the vans.

The four huddled close. The only light at their clandestine meeting was the lantern's glow from inside the tent. Avery whispered about his unexpected visitor. Catherine was unsure if they should trust Sam, but given the questionable vans, something was going to transpire, whatever that was, it would be enacted by the agents, by those present or all of the above. Mistake had never had telepathy prior to the grey cat but had a strong impression they needed ferns for their sculpture. They learned from several newly crowned cat psychic influencers that felines sometimes use mental pictures to communicate. The key caveat would be to less literally interpret the message they received, but Mistake failed to perceive one. Catherine was game to go and get the plants and wondered if the ferns would have something to say about the cat's request.

Avery wanted to scope out the roundabout, and Mistake had the same inclination. Avery intended to warn the orbs but did not mention it. Instead, he studied the way Julia and Catherine held hands. Mistake focused on their hands as well. Catherine was high and did not think Julia or she should drive to the nursery. She stashed Julia in the kitchen and went to see if Evil was up for an adventure.

* * *

"Did you know that ferns are older than dinosaurs?" Julia called from the backseat.

Catherine did not.

The entire evening perturbed Evil. She missed the question and did not care. She pulled into the parking lot. It was empty save for a blue truck that Julia immediately recognized, "That's Patricia's truck. Maybe we should find another spot?"

Evil killed the engine. Julia contemplated staying in the car but did not want to appear childish. Flood lights illuminated separate sections within the outdoor space. It would be easy to locate ferns after-hours. Evil did not want to drive anywhere else. She was still trapped in a never-ending dinner party. Catherine placed her hand on Evil's thigh, "Babe, do you think we should leave cash?"

Evil looked at Catherine's hand and shrugged, "I'm just the getaway car."

All three of them hopped over a thick chain that ran the width of the lot. Slammed by the familiar wave of seasickness, Julia and Catherine were overwhelmed. They drew together and held hands to quell it.

Evil was taken aback.

She whisper-yelled, "You never hold hands."

"Do you really want to process this right now?"

Evil did. It was possibly her breaking point. Julia used her free hand to clasp Evil's hand and then pulled her towards the nursery. It was enough human contact for Evil to let it ride, for the moment.

Pop music played on the nursery's sound system. Mysterious rustling sounds emanated from somewhere near the middle of the shop. Catherine, Evil, and Julia slunk behind a row of shrubs and angled towards the noise. They repositioned behind a table with various types of ground cover. From there, ferns were visible, and so was Patricia dressed in her underwear. She was in the throes of a ritual; a plant lap dance if plants had laps. She held a wine glass filled with water in one hand and bent over to tip water from a second wine glass into the fern's pot. She set both glasses down and giggled.

For a time, they were all too stunned to speak. Julia squeezed Evil's hand. Catherine and Julia both starred at Evil, like Patricia was hers to address. Evil rolled her eyes then cleared her throat. Patricia was surprised and annoyed. She pulled on her clothes, shouting, "We're closed! Obviously. Obviously very much closed! Go away!"

Evil approached instead.

"Patricia, we need your help."

"Evil?"

"Yep."

"For fuck's sake. Hang on."

Patricia beckoned them into a dark garden shed lined with sharp pointy tools. They crowded into the center to avoid being poked. Patricia switched on a small work lamp and closed the doors. Julia tucked herself behind Evil and hoped to go unrecognized. Patricia folded her arms and exhaled impatiently, "What kind of help?"

It was hard to define, but Evil tried, "Things are happening. And you know stuff about the plant-telepathy and military agents and UFOs and UAPs. More stuff than anyone, probably. I thought you might know what to make of this." Evil handed over Mistake's sketch. Patricia studied it.

"Hmm …" She closed them into the shed and disappeared.

Julia experienced an entirely different relationship to the nursery this time. The plants seemed calmer. There was a softer tone, and they seemed to enjoy the music. Julia could not recall if music was playing the last time she was there, but it was during business hours. Perhaps the shuffle of patrons ready to disappear with any plant at any time had put the place on edge. It must be jarring for a plant to experience that kind of constant loss of kin. You could be potted next to a lifelong friend, or even a plant that gave rise to your existence, then poof, it's gone! Were plants exempt from traumatic stress? Julia decided after-hours had far more appeal. It was an after-party, like birds singing at dawn to let each other know that they survived the night. Here, plants celebrated another business day gone by.

Julia and Catherine both experienced a wild hum that vibrated throughout their bodies, as if they had been granted passage to a secret world. Catherine understood something uncomfortably transcendent: everything around her was very much alive. Julia plugged into universal desire, the lusty spawning signals that drove pollination. Erasure's "Always" came on. Julia absent-mindedly stroked Catherine's fingers. Catherine reached for Evil, kissed her, and then turned to kiss Julia. Evil questioned her reality. Catherine put her arms around Evil and Julia and directed them to kiss. Evil and Julia kissed with some reservation, each afraid of some kind of gotcha. Evil's heart pounded. She jumped when Patricia returned with Fern.

"Okay, horny sluts, it's go time."

Evil crossed her arms, "What does that mean?"

"It means let's go. Out of the shed. Follow me."

* * *

The caravan arrived at the roundabout. Evil, Julia, and Catherine all wore matching ugly green nursery vests without a fight. They piled out of the car. Patricia was already parked, and ready with her clipboard. She directed her new workers as they unloaded ferns in cement pots from the back of the blue truck. They worked together to place them onto a cart. Patricia wheeled it over to the roundabout. She directed the placement of the ferns according to Mistake's sketch. Patricia chased off several cats who had contradictory opinions about placement.

Avery and Mistake watched on from a safe distance. Avery patted Mistake's leg to get their attention and pointed to one of two parked vans with dark tinted windows. Jay photographed the plant delivery from the open driver side window. Mistake shrugged then whispered, "The gang's all here."

Avery felt it then. The electric static feeling on hairs all over on his body.

"The orbs are here. I'm going to try to warn them—with my mind."

Mistake was a little incredulous, but given their sudden cat calls, who were they to doubt?

Avery took out his phone and messaged *AlienGuy666*, a teenage girl in Bakersfield who planned to share his live feed with the broader UFO/UAP community. Avery no longer had followers, but the teen could get him fast traction for the video so that it would have legs.

Mistake patted Avery's arm and gestured to the underside of the van. The two of them lowered to the ground to get a better view. Mysterious equipment was fastened to the underside of the van. Metal rods dipped below the tires just off the ground. Avery tapped Mistake's shoulder and pointed at antennas along the van's roof. Mistake nodded. It looked like surveillance gear to the untrained eye. Avery guessed the operatives used whatever intel they gleaned from his time in their custody to draw the orbs to the roundabout. He felt betrayed.

Avery tried desperately to contact the orbs to tell them not to fall for their trap. They were in danger. He tried to transmit the language he learned in his UFO dream—*No Going, No, No, No Going.*

Avery sensed that the orbs were not *no going,* but that they were very much, yes, coming. His shook his head, "I think it's too late. Stubborn obs."

Avery made a break for some bushes near the roundabout to conduct his live feed. He pulled out his phone, taking a moment to consider the consequences of ratting out the operatives. He concluded that he had nothing or everything to lose and might as well press on. The idea that any nation could use weapons and legislation to block human evolution and simply refuse advanced species access to a world, that was also their world, devastated him. He knew how close that contact truly was, and it compelled him to act. He could not tolerate any more mass denial. It was happening, telepathy was real, and humans were capable of communicating with alien life. Most importantly, *he* was able to do it and needed to tell the world about the orbs, once more for the people in the back. Avery went live on his new account, "Hey everyone, I am sorry for my disappearance. There are agents affiliated with the U.S. military that want to eradicate the orbs before we have any meaningful contact. I don't know for certain, but things have gone down and are going down right now. The same orbs are headed over to the roundabout again. I am able to interact with them and I bet you can too." Avery filmed the empty sky but knew it would not disappoint. From the corner of his eye, he saw Mistake lead a procession of cats to the roundabout.

The cats meowed a single, harmonized, guttural sound that was incredibly irritating. Mistake shared a live video on their own account and told everyone to take to the streets to fight against anti-cat psychic legislation. Mistake followed the grey cat's instructions and did not comment on the orbs. They maintained focus on the impressive flood of consciousness-raising felines at their feet, continuing a collective tonal yowl. Mistake understood that the concentrated vibration from the cats would trigger telepathy in those predisposed towards it, like activating a dormant gene. Telepaths were more sensitive to the world and would help clear the way for a more harmonious existence for all living beings, including intergalactic life forms. The cats may have been pulling Mistake's leg, but regardless, the spectacle was undeniably next level.

Julia lost her balance when a sea of cats ran past. Evil caught her as she stumbled, reaching out to steady her. Something had changed between them. Catherine trained her eyes on Mistake, who looked like a cat marching band leader, a phone raised in the air in lieu of a baton. Cats pooled in from different directions, all in a kind of trance as they raced towards the roundabout.

"Those cats are going to fuck up my ferns!" Patricia ran at full speed to protect her potted plants.

Jay spoke into a headset and Xander appeared from the shadows within seconds. They both yanked on the underside of the van as if releasing a couch bed. Xander turned the geometric paddle before them perpendicular to the van and extended it outwards like a fin. The fin vibrated with a low hum.

Avery needed the orbs to leave. He had attempted to multi-task but failed. He had no choice but to delegate the live feed to Evil. He no longer cared if the agents saw him. Avery threaded through a glaring of cats in the throes of a high-pitched wail. He raced across the living obstacle course to get to Evil. Avery brushed against a black cat but stopped short of any real impact. The cat yelled at him anyway. It was just like Avery's dream a few nights prior, and it reminded him of the sketch he made of a cat yelling. Was it a premonition? Did he have it backwards? Had the orbs already shown him this moment? Avery reached Evil and handed her his phone. He was out of breath but managed to communicate that she was in charge of his video, and that it was a very important job. The whole world was watching! Avery broke back into a run towards a nearby yard to exit the chaos. He needed calmer conditions to focus on the orbs.

Evil grabbed Catherine's shoulder, "Holy fuck!" Catherine followed Evil's eye line up to the sky. Orbs circled and zipped around. Evil tried to capture them for Avery's live feed but was overwhelmed, they were absolutely real. They were insanely fast and eerily quiet. A nature photographer would have been a better fit than a portrait artist, but Evil had to do it. She hated recording videos on her phone. Catherine placed her hand on Evil's back to reassure her but refused to take over. Evil committed herself to the task at hand, but still had a hell of a time catching an orb without a wide shot that made them seem tiny.

Julia, who was adept and loved using her phone camera, photographed and recorded videos of Mistake, who was on the plinth covered head to toe in cats. They looked like a dadaist fur-lined sculpture, choreographing with the cats so that they shifted into new poses in perfect sync. It was mesmerizing. The cats incessantly continued to be loud.

The ferns that encircled the roundabout amplified the cats' sound and transformed it into an interspecies signal. The vibration was so powerful it uprooted something within Julia, and her seasickness equalized into a soft manageable hum. She thought it might dissipate entirely, but her reverie broke when several cats attacked one of the ferns. Julia ran to help the plant. The ceaseless meows stopped abruptly. All of the cats suddenly went silent like a line gone dead.

At that precise moment, Evil had one of the orbs framed up on the live feed. A fiery flash exploded in the sky. Two jets roared in a low flying maneuver. It terrified the cats and sent them running in a frenzy. The cats fought each other, hissed, and dashed under cars. Julia saw Patricia bolt and trailed after her. Patricia jumped into her truck and sped off without a word. She nearly ran over several cats, and Julia screamed when the tires got too close to the frightened animals. Julia was no longer seasick but emotionally unmoored.

Xander appeared to have some technical issues with the fin. Jay assisted him. Avery had fallen to his knees. He felt two of the orbs safely in the distance. He sensed that they knew that the jets would fire, they had expected it, and that it was useful. But maybe he was just lying to himself to feel better about the U.S. military shooting down aliens. Shoot first, no questions later. Before Avery blacked out, he saw Sam slip behind a large tree to relieve herself. Her face was in shock, like she was truly surprised that the jets had exploded one of the orbs. What did she think was going to happen?

Evil took advantage of delegating to her assistant and handed Avery's phone to Julia. She asked her to keep recording the orbs on his live feed. Evil turned back and saw Avery seizing on the ground. Catherine was already with him, she turned Avery onto his side and placed her green vest under his head as a pillow. Evil never moved faster in her life.

* * *

The predominant color of the light was white. It vibrated, which altered the temperature to reveal many colors. Avery singled out shades of blue to red to orange and back to white. He felt like a baby experiencing color for the first time, and also like an adult was watching him. Avery was not alone, not in a room. Avery thought about Octavia Butler. He wondered what she would do, or if he had the vision, too, because of her books. He considered artificial intelligence and extraterrestrial intelligence. He preferred the latter. In a funny way, he felt like whatever was with him appreciated that. Avery wanted to ask to interact with god or God or a higher power in some way but was scared to inquire. He did not know if it was benevolent. The odds had not been in his favor as of late. For some reason he knew it was ancient. He wondered if he was dying. He hoped he was no longer on earth.

Avery was wrapped in towels. A familiar voice, the Supervisor, said "Lorazepam?" He knew the smell, the water-lined coffin, something had gone wrong. He was shocked by an electric charge and the tank shut down. It smelled like rotten eggs. Avery had seized. They pulled him out and dried him off with serious speed. They shot him up with more drugs. Foggy again. Avery was on the street with

Catherine and Evil. But he was also in a van with Xander and Jay. Sam drove his car to the parking lot. She must have been the one in charge of wiping his accounts. The one with his phone. NDA. He was back in the present moment. He did not want to return. He kept his eyes shut and tried to stay with his memory. They never finished. Did they get what they needed? Did they bait him to the roundabout and play-act the whole thing like a performance, a show? Was he the only reason the orbs were overhead? Avery wanted to return to the ancient witness who did not mind that he was such a stupid baby. He felt a warm wetness arrive in his crotch and came to.

Catherine and Evil helped Avery stand. He'd peed his pants and was embarrassed. Catherine put her arm around him, and Evil remained vigilant because there were agents nearby. She locked eyes with Jay and Xander who looked back as if she was the threat. Evil flipped them off and yelled, "Fuck you!" Catherine found it endearing and smirked. Once they were settled in the car, Evil rolled down the windows and drove carefully to avoid the cats. Some of the pets made a dash back to their respective households. Glowing eyes and puffy tails appeared in nearly every lawn. A large brown and white fluffball ran across the street trailed by two plump orange cats. Evil swerved. A majestic cat with blue eyes stared them down from the sidewalk. Evil thought the cat was sizing her up; unimpressed, the Persian cat yawned and looked away. Evil asked if she could take Avery to a hospital, but he refused. He said he would go to a walk-in clinic the next day. She would ask Julia to host Mistake for the night. Catherine was in the backseat, concerned that with the windows down she would feel seasick once more, but whatever transpired at the roundabout had revamped her ability to commune with vegetation in a new way. Instead of nonconsensual chatter, she was able to connect and disconnect. She found herself thinking about the oak tree in the distance, and then the oak tree was with her, more than ready to hear all about her night. Catherine was touched. Her world felt bigger. As they pulled into the garage, Evil and Catherine briefly locked eyes in the rear view, a blend of intrigue, heat, and awe.

Avery bolted from the car, plunked the urine-soaked green vest he sat on into the washing machine, and shut the door behind him. The overhead light dimmed until it was pitch black in the garage. It was quiet for a moment. Evil got out of the car and joined Catherine in the backseat. She kissed her neck and pulled her hair. The car made an incessant dinging sound that killed the teenage fantasy. Evil slid out and leaned into the front seat, yanking keys from the ignition. Catherine exited the passenger door and flipped on the light as her body disappeared beyond the threshold. Evil wanted an herbal cigarette.

* * *

In the span of several minutes, agents sped away in their creeper vans and the sky above the roundabout was empty, as if nothing had happened. Julia stopped Avery's live feed and traded out his phone for her own. She was eager to return to Mistake, who was still atop the plinth, covered in scratches. The ones across their forehead and face bled profusely. Julia was captivated by Mistake. Death by a thousand cats. She broke into a light sweat while watching them remove their shirt. Mistake pressed the shirt against the gash in their forehead like an oversized bandage, then waved. Julia was officially smitten and continued to take pictures of them. It was strange to feel enamored in the wake of alien contact and state violence, but she was flooded with adrenaline, ideal for a first date.

Julia heard the frightened ferns cry, "Stop, you unseemly beasts!" She clapped the cats away from their damaged fronds and felt useful to her plant friends for the first time. Mistake called for her. She waited for a second then sauntered over. Mistake drew her up. Julia swooned being close to them on top of the tight platform like they were about to kiss, but Mistake swiveled her around to face oncoming headlights where backlit teenagers in cat masks marched towards the roundabout. Mistake held one arm tight around her waist and recorded the protest. "Do you have a lot of teen followers or something?" Mistake squeezed her hip.

"I just did everything Pepper wanted."

"Pepper?"

"You met. The grey cat from your yard."

"No. You never introduced us."

Julia leaned against their chest and neck. It was then that she spotted two orbs overhead. She reached for Avery's phone to document but decided against it. She sensed they only returned to watch their handiwork unfold and see what happened next. Also, she didn't feel like doing anything more for Avery.

Placards dotted the horizon. People in cat masks marched in as the real cats split. Julia panned the crowd and sent the video to Franklin. Almost immediately her phone swished with a text from Evil asking if she could host Mistake for the night, Avery needed the room. Julia had a sudden change of heart and found she was happy to help Avery out. She texted the letter "k" to Evil.

Julia angled her head to catch a glimpse of Mistake's sexy face and was alarmed by the look of their scratches.

"We should get you back to mine to clean out your wounds."

"I bet you say that to all the thems."

Mistake jumped down then reached for Julia. The plinth was vacant momentarily before the young crowd ascended. Julia checked on the ferns and lost sight of Mistake. She wove through pooling bodies, delighted each time a cat mask turned her way. The protesters thinned out. Julia found Mistake drawing in a tiny notebook. Mistake jotted down one last note, "Ready."

The pair walked home in the middle of the road flanked by flora and fauna, chants of "Whose streets? Our streets!" fading in the distance.

* * *

Julia generously applied newly expired ointment to Mistake's red and swollen brow. Fresh from the shower in the steam filled bathroom, they were dressed only in Franklin's robe. The worst gashes were on Mistake's forearm and shoulders. "You should probably disrobe, like literally take that off. Franklin should have boxers or something." Mistake locked eyes with Julia to keep her in check as they dropped the robe and tied it around their waist. Julia squeezed clear gel across bloodied claw marks and gently rubbed it in. She washed her hands. Mistake hadn't made any advances, but tension remained on a slow cook. As she set down the hand towel, Mistake clasped her jumpsuit zipper for the second time that night.

"It only seems fair."

"I think you'll find I'm more than fair."

Mistake lowered Julia's zipper so slowly by the time they reached the final teeth, she was enflamed. Before Mistake's eager palm met her skin, she clasped the slack arms of their robe and pulled it towards the bedroom like a tight leash. Four hours later, they were dehydrated enough to break for water. They fell asleep after sunrise, only the bottom sheet left on the bed enveloping them in a damp cocoon.

21

Franklin read about the passing of Patti Smith's twenty-one-year-old Abyssinian cat Cairo. It was the first post in his feed. He considered offering condolences in the comments. He wanted to but braving the divide from fiction to real interaction felt like a lesson learned. It also stoked existential dread. Vegas was now a composite character drawn fully from the beyond, her two Scorpio familiars, Mapplethorpe and Cairo.

The Fates loomed heavy. Franklin wondered if weaving Cairo into his fiction was a good or bad thing. He wished he could give something back to Patti, not just pull threads from her reality like he did with real life Henry. He scrolled up with his thumb to draw a clean line. He already felt too close to his characters and troubled by a new post-modern bleed. Julia sent a video, a high angle pan across a crowd of teens in cat masks protesting at his neighborhood roundabout, without any additional context. The video cut out after landing on a handwritten sign, *Cats Have The Power.* Unsurprisingly, Julia was now ignoring his calls and texts. Franklin rejoined social media for clues but felt unsure if he should veer from writing to dive into the mystery.

Phone in hand, he interrupted the screensaver on his laptop and returned to the page. He was midsentence in the final chapter of his manuscript. Jean Cocteau's character, Jean, was president of the local cat lovers club where a number of characters overlapped: Yoko, Jean-Michel, and Frida were prominent members. Andy's membership had been revoked. In this late chapter, Cocteau's Siamese cats, Paul and Elisabeth, assumed club leadership after luring those in attendance into a telepathic trance to share psychic bonds as part of their little game. Siamese cats are known for being chatty; Paul was quite the orator going on about his father's rough treatment and abandonment. Elisabeth then upstaged her brother by breaking into Cat Power's "Bathysphere," Yoko, joining in on the chorus. Franklin stared at the blinking cursor.

He wanted to live in a bathysphere ever since he heard Cat Power's record in the late '90s. It was so relatable. His father Leonard had also crushed his soul when he was seven, just like the one in the song. Franklin's father later drowned in the sea in an unexpected reprise. He had achieved a bathyspheresque lifestyle in many regards, adrift in a solitary writing studio with a view, for one. Years ago, he stood in a check-out line behind Chan Marshall at a small natural market in Los Angeles. She was buying seaweed snacks and it felt like the perfect segue to say something about loving "Bathysphere." Out of respect and his own insecurity, Franklin pretended not to recognize the musician but spent the rest of the afternoon daydreaming about a conversation they didn't have. He wondered if stage fright was similar to gender dysphoria because that seemed to track, not wanting to perform and all. He would not have known the phrase "gender dysphoria" at that time, but it's the closest language has gotten to what he would have meant.

Software blocked Franklin's laptop from accessing the internet during work hours, so he cheated with his phone. He caught up on the so-called cat psychic teen take over and subsequent anti-cat psychic campaigns. There were already two hundred bills circulating across the U.S. written by a handful of unbearable quacks. Delving into the online fray, Franklin struggled to understand the concerns around animal communicators—it was not new. Animal messages arrived in quotidian dreams and omens dating back to the start of life on earth. Cave art reflected as much. People communicated with their pets all the time, in most cultures, psychic or not. Who wasn't at least a little telepathic? Franklin lost interest in whatever was happening back home. He was about to set down his phone when he noticed Henry and Edith hosting a live stream.

* * *

Edith was enjoying their new variety show but was loath to admit it. She mewed into the camera while Henry, dressed in a thrifted Comme des Garçon button down, fake-clutched his imaginary pearls.

"Edith, are you really taking credit for inspiring tang ping, or the lying flat movement, AND quiet-quitting?"

Edith's black tail curled above her innocent face. She chirped a sassy meow that sounded exactly like, "Okay" and slow-blinked into the lens. With UFOs still at a remove, cats and plants were two of the most manipulative beings on the planet—#notallcats—and now they had more influence than ever before. One of them was bound to run with it.

Acknowledgments

This book would not exist without my editor, publisher, artistic collaborator, and astounding friend, Michelle Tea. I am immensely grateful to Michelle, as well as Beth Pickens, Hedi El Kholti, Faye Orlove, Katie Fricas, DOPAMINE Press and Semiotext(e).

The title emerged from a chat with my best friend, collaborator and guiding luminary, Larry Arrington. *New Mistakes* was inspired by chatty flora, fauna, and extra-terrestrials in the neighborhood of Mount Washington on unceded Chumash/Tongva land. My tuxedo familiar Cazimi served as both muse and cat consultant.

Writing was anchored by weekly Mercury work sessions with Veronica Gonzalez Peña, Naz Riahi, and friends. Thanks to my family of origin especially my sister Jody, Mom and Michael, the Greenbergs, and ones that are no longer here.

This novel, like most of my practice, is a love letter to my queer and trans artist community and lineage. My place in this world is only possible because of you.

There are a few super antennas I want to thank, Miguel Mendías, Dia Felix, Silas Howard, Julián Delgado Lopera, Maryam Rostami, Jackson Bowman, Steven Reigns, Guinevere Turner, Bett Williams, Zackary Drucker, Gail DeKosnik, Melodie Sisk, Meredith Singer, Michelle Martens, Ted Metzger, Tina DiGeorge, Jenny Walters, Gabriel Cameron, Alison Kelly, James Fleming, Harris Kornstein, Tanya Wiscerath, Heather María Ács, Beth Hill, Irina Contreras, Xandra Ibarra, Brontez Purnell, Ron Athey, Virgie Tovar, Kirk Read, Amber Dawn, Lisa Brown, Bay Area / LA art and queer fam, and friends of Dorotheus.

.

ABOUT THE AUTHOR

Clement Goldberg is an award-winning multidisciplinary artist, writer, director, and animator who is non-binary trans and queer. They work across disciplines to create satirical yet hopeful projects. Clement received a 2022 Creative Capital Award for their sci-fi comedy feature film, *Let Me Let You Go*. Their work has been presented at venues such as The Broad Museum, REDCAT Theatre, BAMPFA, Institute of Contemporary Art Philadelphia, and over fifty international film and arts festivals. Clement was awarded a Creative Work Fund visual arts grant in collaborative partnership with CounterPulse for *Our Future Ends* "a fifty-minute masterpiece of surrealist political satire"—*LA WEEKLY*, about near-extinct lemurs and long-lost Lemuria. Goldberg created the stop-motion animated series *The Deer Inbetween* and joined Michelle Tea to produce the award-winning twenty-filmmaker omnibus adaptation of Tea's iconic memoir, *Valencia*. Clement received an MFA in Art Practice from the University of California, Berkeley.

clemgoldberg.com